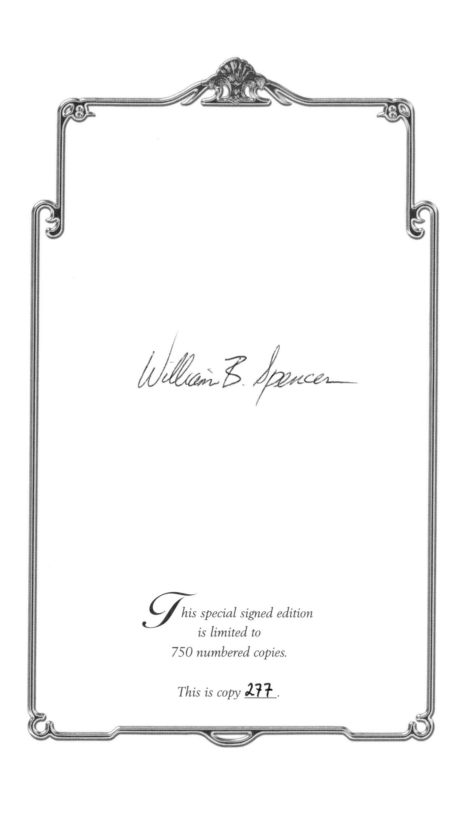

William B. Spencer

The
Ocean
and
All Its Devices

The
Ocean
and
All Its Devices

Stories by
William Browning Spencer

Subterranean Press 2006

Table of Contents

This book is dedicated to Liz, my wife,
and Amoreena, my meditation coach.

Introduction

A WRITER IS A PERSON WHO HAS FOUND
A WAY OF TALKING AT GREAT LENGTH
WITHOUT BEING INTERRUPTED…

*E*very now and then, I'll hear someone say that the mountain dulcimer is on the way out, that it can't compete with the electric guitar, that it has failed to find a place in hip-hop or rap, that it has no relevance in the angry, sampled sounds of urban angst. Such doomsayers are always with us. These folks are kin to those who tell us short fiction is finished. I say to them, "Hah! What do you know? Get out of here!"

But some days I wonder. Just a couple of weeks ago, I read in the *New York Times Book Review* that magazine editors were cutting back on fiction or chucking it entirely. Fiction, it seems, just isn't that relevant in an event-filled world in need of a logical narrative.

And why read any fiction, for that matter? If you feel the need for a story, you can watch one. You own a television, don't you? Why run your mind ragged, bouncing over one stony, demanding sentence after another, besieged by images that you—*yourself!*—have to conjure up (no remuneration for this, no thanks from the author for generating these internal visuals on your own time) when you can watch television? TV is such a friend to the weary; it doesn't ask much, and, like

9

a ne'er-do-well uncle, it has lost its capacity to disappoint. Nothing much is expected of television, and so it offers a level of comfort denied to art with greater aspirations.

I once wrote a short story entitled *Haunted by the Horror King*, in which the narrator, a failed novelist, is slowly going crazy in the shadow of Stephen King's success. Among other things, the narrator believes that his wife is sleeping with the famous author. I chose Stephen King as the celebrity writer whose fame and success drive my hero around the bend because I was familiar with his work, but any hugely popular writer of fiction would have served my purpose. How does the ignored writer dodge envy and bitterness? How does he keep clear of the thought that he is writing in a vacuum, making no real sound as he topples over in the forest? Is he as deluded as some drug-addled blogger alone in a room with his computer and the cast-off shells of ordered-out pizzas, ranting to a potential audience of millions (because they are irrefutably out there; those millions of readers are out there on the Web)? Is he impervious to self-doubt, and, if not, does he rally with self-affirmations or does he lose himself to the tawdry blandishments of despair? Am I the only one who thinks John Kennedy Toole might still be alive if Robert Gottlieb at Simon & Schuster hadn't spent two years of editorial obtuseness mulling over *A Confederacy of Dunces* in unhelpful letters before rejecting it? Granted, suicide is an extreme reaction. But what writer hasn't felt a sinking sensation when it becomes clear that the editor/publisher whose judgment will determine the fate of his novel is completely devoid of the sensibility required to understand it?

Of course, to be really put out by the success of others, you have to believe that you deserve the accolades they are receiving. You have to believe that you are an authentic genius, doomed by circumstances and fools to languish in neglect while lesser talents thrive. From all I know of other writers and from my own study of myself, I suspect that all writers are convinced they are not properly appreciated. Herman Melville wrote *Moby-Dick*, and nobody bought it, although he had been doing fairly well as a novelist before that. *M-D* bombed big time, and Melville wound up working as a customs inspector, and you know he must have seethed every time some co-worker said, "I have got to say I'm not surprised, Herman. There's only so much people want to know about whales, and you went way over the limit." And Melville would have had to sit there stewing, silently swallowing these facile critiques. You can't argue with rotten sell-through. As a consequence of his novel's dismal sales, Melville had a nervous breakdown and was so reduced by his misfortune that he could write nothing but poetry in the last years of his life, a condition I would not wish on anyone.

What do you do when your art fails to earn you a living? Well, there is a martyr's consolation in being misunderstood and ignored. Poverty is every writer's proof of his integrity and of the high seriousness of his art. There's a powerful, perverse thrill in sharing tales of artistic squalor with other writers. Gambling on fiction, I've lost everything many times, although—I love saying this—it's only been about twenty dollars.

In 1998, Gordon Van Gelder, my editor at St. Martin's Press, sent me a collection of Howard Waldrop's short stories, *Going Home Again*. Mr. Waldrop writes strange, brilliant, idiosyncratic stories that garner rave reviews. Waldrop fans tend to be fanatical in their devotion. When I attended a World Fantasy Convention in Baltimore some years ago, the line of readers clutching books to be signed was longest in front of Howard Waldrop's table. But single-author short story collections are not big sellers. Howard Waldrop, in his introduction to *Going Home Again*, notes that writing short stories, which is primarily what he does, is not a road to great wealth. He writes of living in a shack in the wilderness with $4.80 in the bank, of receiving a royalty check for $1.92, which he is unable to cash because he has no gas for his car, and his bank is 15 miles away. He writes of living for four days on berries he foraged along the riverbank.

Reading Howard Waldrop's introduction took the wind out of my sails. There was no getting around it. I was a dilettante, a man whose trials were laughable: a car without air-conditioning, fast food instead of a restaurant's cuisine, creditors on the phone. Were those things true adversity? Hardly. I couldn't look my Muse in the eye. She had read Howard Waldrop's intro over my shoulder, and I was now the subject of her cold appraisal. Mine was a lukewarm ardor, and my Muse was wondering what she had seen in me. She never said it, but I could hear her thinking: *How many days would you live off berries for my favors?*

The company of other writers can be a solace. A writers' group in Austin was the main reason I began writing short stories. The short stories were fun to read at meetings. There can, however, be a downside to these feedback groups. Some people are inhibited by the often fierce and unforgiving attention of other writers. One woman I knew was so cowed by the criticism of her colleagues that she labored for over a year on a single short story, never, to my knowledge, completing it, never submitting it for the group's critical consideration. She left the group in a huff when a writer of short horror fiction (a retired civil engineer and a published writer with stories in magazines like *Splatter, Tales of Disembowelment*, and *Queasy Worlds*) advised her to tell people she was working on a novel. Laboring over a short story for over a year, he suggested, might look like some kind of mental problem, while you could wrestle with a novel for decades and still be taken seriously.

When my first short story collection was published, every story in it was appearing for the first time. I hadn't been able to sell a single one of them, and I had tried. *All* of the stories in the present collection were previously sold to magazines and anthologies. That's progress. I could probably sell a few more short stories if I weren't working on a novel that (see above) seems like a better excuse for my feckless lifestyle.

Perhaps I will never write another short story. With the appearance of this collection, all the short stories I have ever written are in book form. That appeals to my sense of neatness and order. Were I to write more short stories, these new ones would be strewn about, accumulating in the past, a literary flotsam and jetsam with no coherent theme or style or direction home. Just a lot of scrabbling fiefdoms hanging on to life as time pushed them inexorably under.

Or maybe I'll suddenly see the short story as the only viable way to confront the world, and I'll write as many as the remaining years allow. I don't know how life is for others, but I often see myself as a person whose actions are tentative and subject to the whim of inscrutable impulses. Years ago, during a period when I was lying fallow, a friend said, "Do you suppose you'll ever write another novel?"

I answered, "I hope so," realizing by his reaction to my words that the rest of the world may feel more in charge than I do. I am often the observer, several feet to the left and twenty feet off the ground, watching myself drift down the street, thinking, "I hope he'll do the right thing," but not at all sure that he will.

And if my own bad impulses don't sabotage me, there is always irony. Irony has a particular affinity for writers. I once had an agent who stated in a letter to me that he had been a great help to Philip K. Dick while admitting that most of that help had come after Mr. Dick's death. Posterity loves to mess with authors after they are gone, exalting them or obliterating them.

We are all terrifyingly mortal, despite the way words can make us feel so powerful, so out of range. My friend, fellow Austin writer Glen Alyn, wrote on my copy of his book, *I Say Me for a Parable*, "Well, here we are. On the precipice of eternity? I'm banking on success for the both of us." Glen was killed in a car accident, eternity claiming him while fame eluded him.

The novelist Richard Fariña, who was also a folksinger/songwriter in 1965 when folksinger/songwriter didn't, somehow, sound like an oxymoron, was killed in a motorcycle accident two days after the publication of his novel, *Been Down So Long It Looks Like Up to Me*. His book promised great things—as did his music.

On the albums that he recorded with his wife, Mimi Fariña (Joan Baez's sister), Richard Fariña's instrument of choice was the mountain dulcimer. Could there be malign, invisible forces marshaled against the mountain dulcimer? Are these same forces now threatening the short story? Who can say?

I had hoped for more coherence in this intro, but it is best to move on sometimes. Moving on: I want to thank my readers, those people who have let me know, over the years, that they were listening, that they were out there somewhere immersed in my books, reading them with real pleasure, *enjoying* them, and allowing me to ramble on, uninterrupted.

P.S. A note to fans who might write me: All praise is negated if a letter begins, "I read a portion of your story collection, and I thought it was rather good and quite a bit like what I do. I am a writer myself, and I have been unsuccessful in acquiring an agent. I wouldn't be surprised if your agent would enjoy my work, since we both..."

The Ocean
and All Its Devices

Left to its own enormous devices the sea
in timeless reverie conceives of life,
being itself the world in pantomime.

—LLOYD FRANKENBERG, *The Sea*

*T*he hotel's owner and manager, George Hume, sat on the edge of his bed and smoked a cigarette. "The Franklins arrived today," he said.

"Regular as clockwork," his wife said.

George nodded. "Eight years now. And why? Why ever do they come?"

George Hume's wife, an ample woman with soft, motherly features, sighed. "They seem to get no pleasure from it, that's for certain. Might as well be a funeral they come for."

The Franklins always arrived in late fall, when the beaches were cold and empty and the ocean, under dark skies, reclaimed its terrible majesty. The hotel was almost deserted at this time of year, and George had suggested closing early for the winter. Mrs. Hume had said, "The Franklins will be coming, dear."

So what? George might have said. Let them find other accommodations this year. But he didn't say that. They were sort of a tradition, the Franklins, and in a world so fraught with change, one just naturally protected the rare, enduring pattern.

They were a reserved family who came to this quiet hotel in North Carolina like refugees seeking safe harbor. George couldn't close early and send the Franklins off to some inferior establishment. Lord, they might wind up at The Cove with its garish lagoon pool and gaudy tropical lounge. That wouldn't suit them at all.

The Franklins (husband, younger wife, and pale, delicate-featured daughter) would dress rather formally and sit in the small opened section of the dining room—the rest of the room shrouded in dust covers while Jack, the hotel's aging waiter and handyman, would stand off to one side with a bleak, stoic expression.

Over the years George had come to know many of his regular guests well. But the Franklins had always remained aloof and enigmatic. Mr. Greg Franklin was a man in his mid or late forties, a handsome man, tall—over six feet— with precise, slow gestures and an oddly uninflected voice, as though he were reading from some internal script that failed to interest him. His much younger wife was stunning, her hair massed in brown ringlets, her eyes large and luminous and containing something like fear in their depths. She spoke rarely, and then in a whisper, preferring to let her husband talk.

Their child, Melissa, was a dark-haired girl—twelve or thirteen now, George guessed—a girl as pale as the moon's reflection in a rain barrel. Always dressed impeccably, she was as quiet as her mother, and George had the distinct impression, although he could not remember being told this by anyone, that she was sickly, that some traumatic infant's illness had almost killed her and so accounted for her methodical, wounded economy of motion.

George ushered the Franklins from his mind. It was late. He extinguished his cigarette and walked over to the window. Rain blew against the glass, and lightning would occasionally illuminate the white-capped waves.

"Is Nancy still coming?" Nancy, their daughter and only child, was a senior at Duke University. She had called the week before saying she might come and hang out for a week or two.

"As far as I know," Mrs. Hume said. "You know how she is. Everything on a whim. That's your side of the family, George."

George turned away from the window and grinned. "Well, I can't accuse your family of ever acting impulsively— although it would do them a world of good. Your family packs a suitcase to go to the grocery store."

"And your side steals a car and goes to California without a toothbrush or a prayer."

This was an old, well-worked routine, and they indulged it as they readied for bed. Then George turned off the light and the darkness brought silence.

It was still raining in the morning when George Hume woke. The violence of last night's thunderstorm had been replaced by a slow, business-like drizzle. Looking out the window, George saw the Franklins walking on the beach under black umbrellas. They were a cheerless sight. All three of them wore dark raincoats, and they might have been fugitives from some old Bergman film, inevitably tragic, moving slowly across a stark landscape.

When most families went to the beach, it was a more lively affair.

George turned away from the window and went into the bathroom to shave. As he lathered his face, he heard the boom of a radio, rock music blaring from the adjoining room, and he assumed, correctly, that his twenty-one-year-old daughter Nancy had arrived as planned.

Nancy had not come alone. "This is Steve," she said when her father sat down at the breakfast table.

Steve was a very young man—the young were getting younger—with a wide-eyed, waxy expression and a blond mustache that looked like it could be wiped off with a damp cloth.

Steve stood up and said how glad he was to meet Nancy's father. He shook George's hand enthusiastically, as though they had just struck a lucrative deal.

"Steve's in law school," Mrs. Hume said, with a proprietary delight that her husband found grating.

Nancy was complaining. She had, her father thought, always been a querulous girl, at odds with the way the world was.

"I can't believe it," she was saying. "The whole mall is closed. The only—and I mean only—thing around here that is open is that cheesy little drugstore, and nobody actually buys anything in there. I know that, because I recognize stuff from when I was six. Is this some holiday I don't know about or what?"

"Honey, it's the off season. You know everything closes when the tourists leave."

"Not the for-Christ-sakes mall!" Nancy said. "I can't believe it." Nancy frowned. "This must be what Russia is like," she said, closing one eye as smoke from her cigarette slid up her cheek.

George Hume watched his daughter gulp coffee. She was not a person who needed stimulants. She wore an ancient gray sweater and sweatpants. Her blonde hair was chopped short and ragged and kept in a state of disarray by the constant furrowing of nervous fingers. She was, her father thought, a pretty girl in disguise.

That night, George discovered that he could remember nothing of the spy novel he was reading, had forgotten, in fact, the hero's name. It was as though he had stumbled into a cocktail party in the wrong neighborhood, all strangers to him, the gossip meaningless.

He put the book on the nightstand, leaned back on the pillow, and said. "This is her senior year. Doesn't she have classes to attend?"

His wife said nothing.

He sighed. "I suppose they are staying in the same room."

"Dear, I don't know," Mrs. Hume said. "I expect it is none of our business."

"If it is not our business who stays in our hotel, then who in the name of hell's business is it?"

Mrs. Hume rubbed her husband's neck. "Don't excite yourself, dear. You know what I mean. Nancy is a grown-up, you know."

George did not respond to this and Mrs. Hume, changing the subject, said, "I saw Mrs. Franklin and her daughter out walking on the beach again today. I don't know where Mr. Franklin was. It was pouring, and there they were, mother and daughter. You know…" Mrs. Hume paused. "It's like they were waiting for something to come out of the sea. Like a vigil they were keeping. I've thought it before, but the notion was particularly strong today. I looked out past them, and there seemed no separation between the sea and the sky, just a black wall of water." Mrs. Hume looked at herself in the dresser's mirror, as though her reflection might clarify matters. "I've lived by the ocean all my life, and I've just taken it for granted, George. Suddenly it gave me the shivers. Just for a moment. I thought, Lord, how big it is, lying there cold and black, like some creature that has slept at your feet so long you never expect it to wake, have forgotten that it might be brutal, even vicious."

"It's all this rain," her husband said, hugging her and drawing her to him. "It can make a person think some black thoughts."

George left off worrying about his daughter and her young man's living arrangements, and in the morning, when Nancy and Steve appeared for breakfast, George didn't broach the subject—not even to himself.

Later that morning, he watched them drive off in Steve's shiny sports car—rich parents, lawyers themselves?—bound for Wilmington and shopping malls that were open.

The rain had stopped, but dark, massed clouds over the ocean suggested that this was a momentary respite. As George studied the beach, the Franklins came into view. They marched directly toward him, up and over the dunes, moving in a soldierly, clipped fashion. Mrs. Franklin was holding her daughter's hand and moving at a brisk pace, almost a run, while her husband faltered behind, his gait hesitant, as though uncertain of the wisdom of catching up.

Mrs. Franklin reached the steps and marched up them, her child tottering in tow, her boot heels sounding hollowly on the wood planks. George nodded, and she passed without speaking, seemed not to see him. In any event, George Hume would have been unable to speak. He was accustomed to the passive, demure countenance of this self-possessed woman, and the expression on her face, a wild distorting emotion, shocked and confounded him. It was an unreadable emotion, but its intensity was extraordinary and unsettling.

George had not recovered from the almost physical assault of Mrs. Franklin's emotional state, when her husband came up the stairs, nodded curtly, muttered something, and hastened after his wife.

George Hume looked after the retreating figures. Mr. Greg Franklin's face had been a mask of cold civility, none of his wife's passion written there, but the man's appearance was disturbing in its own way. Mr. Franklin had been soaking wet, his hair plastered to his skull, his overcoat dripping, the reek of salt water enfolding him like a shroud.

George walked on down the steps and out to the beach. The ocean was always some consolation, a quieting influence, but today it seemed hostile.

The sand was still wet from the recent rains and the footprints of the Franklins were all that marred the smooth expanse. George saw that the Franklins had walked down the beach along the edge of the tide and returned at a greater distance from the water. He set out in the wake of their footprints, soon lost to his own thoughts. He thought about his daughter, his wild Nancy, who had always been boy-crazy. At least this one didn't have a safety-pin through his ear or play in a rock band. *So lighten up*, George advised himself.

He stopped. The tracks had stopped. Here is where the Franklins turned and headed back to the hotel, walking higher up the beach, closer to the weedy debris-laden dunes.

But it was not the ending of the trail that stopped George's own progress down the beach. In fact, he had forgotten that he was absently following the Franklins' spore.

It was the litter of dead fish that stopped him. They were scattered at his feet in the tide. Small ghost crabs had already found the corpses and were laying their claims.

There might have been a hundred bodies. It was difficult to say, for not one of the bodies was whole. They had been hacked into many pieces, diced by some impossibly sharp blade that severed a head cleanly, flicked off a tail or dorsal fin. Here a scaled torso still danced in the sand, there a pale eye regarded the sky.

Crouching in the sand, George examined the bodies. He stood up, finally, as the first large drops of rain plunged from the sky. No doubt some fishermen had called it a day, tossed their scissored bait and gone home.

That this explanation did not satisfy George Hume was the result of a general sense of unease. *Too much rain.*

It rained sullenly and steadily for two days during which time George saw little of his daughter and her boyfriend. Nancy apparently had the young man on a strict regime of shopping, tourist attractions, and movies, and she was undaunted by the weather.

The Franklins kept inside, appearing briefly in the dining room for bodily sustenance and then retreating again to their rooms. And whatever did they do there? Did they play solitaire? Did they watch old reruns on TV?

On the third day, the sun came out, brazen, acting as though it had never been gone, but the air was colder. The Franklins, silhouetted like black crows on a barren field, resumed their shoreline treks.

Nancy and Steve rose early and were gone from the house before George arrived at the breakfast table. George spent the day endeavoring to satisfy the IRS's notion of a small businessman's obligations, and he was in a foul mood by dinner time.

After dinner, he tried to read, this time choosing a much-touted novel that proved to be about troubled youth. He was asleep within fifteen minutes of opening the book and awoke in an overstuffed armchair. The room was chilly, and his wife had tucked a quilt around his legs before abandoning him for bed. In the morning she would, he was certain, assure him that she had tried to rouse him before retiring, but he had no recollection of such an attempt.

"Half a bottle of wine might have something to do with that," she would say.

He would deny the charge.

The advantage of being married a long time was that one could argue without the necessity of the other's actual, physical presence.

He smiled at this thought and pushed himself out of the

chair, feeling groggy, head full of prickly flannel. He looked out the window. It was raining again—to the accompaniment of thunder and explosive, strobe-like lightening. The sports car was gone. The kids weren't home yet. Fine. Fine. None of my business.

Climbing the stairs, George paused. Something dark lay on the carpeted step, and as he bent over it, leaning forward, his mind sorted and discarded the possibilities: cat, wig, bird's nest, giant dust bunny. Touch and a strong olfactory cue identified the stuff: seaweed. Raising his head, he saw that two more clumps of the wet, rubbery plant lay on ascending steps, and gathering them—with no sense of revulsion for he was used to the ocean's disordered presence—he carried the weed up to his room and dumped it in the bathroom's wastebasket.

He scrubbed his hands in the sink, washing away the salty, stagnant reek, left the bathroom and crawled into bed beside his sleeping wife. He fell asleep immediately and was awakened later in the night with a suffocating sense of dread, a sure knowledge that an intruder had entered the room.

The intruder proved to be an odor, a powerful stench of decomposing fish, rotting vegetation and salt water. He climbed out of bed, coughing.

The source of this odor was instantly apparent and he swept up the wastebasket, preparing to gather the seaweed and flush it down the toilet.

The seaweed had melted into a black liquid, bubbles forming on its surface, a dark, gelatinous muck, simmering like heated tar. As George stared at the mess, a bubble burst, and the noxious gas it unleashed dazed him, sent him reeling backward with an inexplicable vision of some monstrous, shadowy form, silhouetted against green, mottled water.

George pitched himself forward, gathered the wastebasket in his arms, and fled the room. In the hall he wrenched open a window and hurled the wastebasket and its contents into the rain.

He stood then, gasping, the rain savage and cold on his face, his undershirt soaked, and he stood that way, clutching the window sill, until he was sure he would not faint.

Returning to bed, he found his wife still sleeping soundly and he knew, immediately, that he would say nothing in the morning, that the sense of suffocation, of fear, would seem unreal, its source irrational. Already the moment of panic was losing its reality, fading into the realm of nightmare.

The next day the rain stopped again and this time the sun was not routed. The police arrived on the third day of clear weather.

Mrs. Hume had opened the door, and she shouted up to her husband, who stood on the landing. "It's about Mr. Franklin."

Mrs. Franklin came out of her room then, and George Hume thought he saw the child behind her, through the open door. The girl, Melissa, was lying on the bed behind her mother and just for a moment it seemed that there was a spreading shadow under her, as though the bedclothes were soaked with dark water. Then the door closed as Mrs. Franklin came into the hall and George identified the expression he had last seen in her eyes for it was there again: fear, a racing engine of fear, gears stripped, the accelerator flat to the floor.

And Mrs. Franklin screamed, screamed and came falling to her knees and screamed again, prescient in her grief, and collapsed as George rushed toward her and two police officers and a paramedic, a woman, came bounding up the stairs.

Mr. Franklin had drowned. A fisherman had discovered the body. Mr. Franklin had been fully dressed, lying on his back with his eyes open. His wallet—and seven hundred dollars in cash and a host of credit cards—was still in his back pocket, and a business card identified him as vice president of marketing for a software firm in Fairfax, Virginia. The police had telephoned Franklin's firm in Virginia and so learned that he was on vacation. The secretary had the hotel's number.

After the ambulance left with Mrs. Franklin, they sat in silence until the police officer cleared his throat and said, "She seemed to be expecting something like this."

The words dropped into a silence.

Nancy and Steve and Mrs. Hume were seated on one of the lobby's sofas. George Hume came out of the office in the wake of the other policeman who paused at the door and spoke. "We'd appreciate it if you could come down and identify the body. Just a formality, but it's not a job for his wife, not in the state she's in." He coughed, shook his head. "Or the state he's in, for that matter. Body got tore up some in the water, and, well, I still find it hard to believe that he was alive just yesterday. I would have guessed he'd been in the water two weeks minimum—the deterioration, you know."

George Hume shook his head as though he did know and agreed to accompany the officer back into town.

George took a long look, longer than he wanted to, but the body wouldn't let him go, made mute, undeniable demands.

Yes, this was Mr. Greg Franklin. Yes, this would make eight years that he and his wife and his child had come to the hotel. No, no nothing out of the ordinary

George interrupted himself. "The tattoos…" he said.

"Didn't know about the tattoos, I take it?" the officer said.

George shook his head. "No." The etched blue lines that laced the dead man's arms and chest were somehow more frightening than the damage the sea had done. Frightening because…because the reserved Mr. Franklin, businessman and stolid husband, did not look like someone who would illuminate his flesh with arcane symbols, pentagrams and ornate fish, their scales numbered according to some runic logic, and spidery, incomprehensible glyphs.

"Guess Franklin wasn't inclined to wear a bathing suit."

"No."

"Well, we are interested in those tattoos. I guess his wife knew about them. Hell, maybe she has some of her own."

"Have you spoken to her?"

"Not yet. Called the hospital. They say she's sleeping. It can wait till morning."

An officer drove George back to the hotel, and his wife greeted him at the door.

"She's sleeping," Mrs. Hume said.

"Who?"

"Melissa."

For a moment, George drew a blank, and then he nodded. "What are we going to do with her?"

"Why, keep her," his wife said. "Until her mother is out of the hospital."

"Maybe there are relatives," George said, but he knew, saying it, that the Franklins were self-contained, a single unit, a closed universe.

His wife confirmed this. No one could be located, in any event.

"Melissa may not be aware that her father is dead," Mrs. Hume said. "The child is, I believe, a stranger girl than we ever realized. Here we were thinking she was just a quiet thing, well behaved. I think there is something wrong with her mind. I can't seem to talk to her, and what she says makes no sense. I've called Dr. Gowers, and he has agreed to see her. You remember Dr. Gowers, don't you? We sent Nancy to him when she was going through that bad time at thirteen."

George remembered child psychiatrist Gowers as a bearded man with a swollen nose and thousands of small wrinkles around his eyes. He had seemed a very kind but somehow sad man, a little like Santa Claus if Santa Claus had suffered some disillusioning experience, an unpleasant divorce or other personal setback, perhaps.

Nancy came into the room as her mother finished speaking. "Steve and I can take Melissa," Nancy said.

"Well, that's very good of you, dear," her mother said. "I've already made an appointment for tomorrow morning at ten. I'm sure Dr. Gowers will be delighted to see you again."

"I'll go too," George said. He couldn't explain it but he was suddenly afraid.

The next morning when George came down to breakfast, Melissa was already seated at the table and Nancy was combing the child's hair.

"She isn't going to church," George said, surprised at the growl in his voice.

"This is what she wanted to wear," Nancy said. "And it looks very nice, I think."

Melissa was dressed in the sort of outfit a young girl might wear on Easter Sunday: a navy blue dress with white trim, white knee socks, black, shiny shoes. She had even donned pale blue gloves. Her black hair had been brushed to a satin sheen and her pale face seemed just-scrubbed, with the scent of soap lingering over her. A shiny black purse sat next to her plate of eggs and toast.

"You look very pretty," George Hume said.

Melissa nodded, a sharp snap of the head, and said, "I am an angel."

Nancy laughed and hugged the child. George raised his eyebrows. "No false modesty here," he said. At least she could talk.

On the drive into town, Steve sat in the passenger seat while George drove. Nancy and Melissa sat in the back seat. Nancy spoke to the child in a slow, reassuring murmur.

Steve said nothing, sitting with his hands in his lap, looking out the window. *Might not be much in a crisis*, George thought. *A rich man's child.*

Steve stayed in the waiting room while the receptionist ushered Melissa and Nancy and George into Dr. Gowers' office. The psychiatrist seemed much as George remembered him, a silver-maned, benign old gent, exuding an air of competence. He asked them to sit on the sofa.

The child perched primly on the sofa, her little black purse cradled in her lap. She was flanked by George and Nancy.

Dr. Gowers knelt down in front of her. "Well, Melissa. Is it all right if I call you Melissa?"

"Yes sir. That's what everyone calls me."

"Well, Melissa, I'm glad you could come and see me today. I'm Dr. Gowers."

"Yes sir."

"I'm sorry about what happened to your father," he said, looking in her eyes.

"Yes sir," Melissa said. She leaned forward and touched her shoe.

"Do you know what happened to your father?" Dr. Gowers asked.

Melissa nodded her head and continued to study her shoes.

"What happened to your father?" Dr. Gowers asked.

"The machines got him," Melissa said. She looked up at the doctor. "The real machines," she added. "The ocean ones."

"Your father drowned," Dr. Gowers said.

Melissa nodded. "Yes sir." Slowly the little girl got up and began wandering around the room. She walked past a large saltwater aquarium next to a teak bookcase.

George thought the child must have bumped against the aquarium stand—although she hardly seemed close enough—because water spilled from the tank as she passed. She was humming. It was a bright, musical little tune, and he had heard it before, a children's song, perhaps? The words? Something like *by the sea, by the sea.*

The girl walked and gestured with a liquid motion that was oddly sophisticated, suggesting the calculated body language of an older and sexually self-assured woman.

"Melissa, would you come and sit down again so we can talk? I want to ask you some questions, and that is hard to do if you are walking around the room."

"Yes sir," Melissa said, returning to the sofa and resettling between George and his daughter. Melissa retrieved her purse and placed it on her lap again.

She looked down at the purse and up again. She smiled with a child's cunning. Then, very slowly, she opened the purse and showed it to Dr. Gowers.

"Yes?" he said, raising an eyebrow.

"There's nothing in it," Melissa said. "It's empty." She giggled.

"Well yes, it is empty," Dr. Gowers said, returning the child's smile. "Why is that?"

Melissa snapped the purse closed. "Because my real purse isn't here. It's in the real place, where I keep my things."

"And where is that, Melissa?"

Melissa smiled and said, "You know, silly."

When the session ended, George phoned his wife.

"I don't know," he said. "I guess it went fine. I don't know. I've had no experience of this sort of thing. What about Mrs. Franklin?"

Mrs. Franklin was still in the hospital. She wanted to leave, but the hospital was reluctant to let her. She was still in shock, very disoriented. She seemed, indeed, to think that it was her daughter who had drowned.

"Did you talk to her?" George asked.

"Well yes, just briefly, but as I say, she made very little sense, got very excited when it became clear I wasn't going to fetch her if her doctor wanted her to remain there."

"Can you remember anything she said?"

"Well, it was very jumbled, really. Something about a bad bargain. Something about, that Greek word, you know 'hubris.'"

"Hewbris?"

"Oh, back in school, you know, George. Hubris. A willful sort of pride that angers the gods. I'm sure you learned it in school yourself."

"You are not making any sense," he said, suddenly exasperated—and frightened.

"Well," his wife said, "you don't have to shout. Of course I don't make any sense. I am trying to repeat what Mrs. Franklin said, and that poor woman made no sense at all. I tried to reassure her that Melissa was fine and she screamed. She said Melissa was not fine at all and that I was a fool. Now you are shouting me, too."

George apologized, said he had to be going, and hung up.

On the drive back from Dr. Gowers' office, Nancy sat in the back seat with Melissa. The child seemed unusually excited: her pale forehead was beaded with sweat, and she watched the ocean with great intensity.

"Did you like Dr. Gowers?" Nancy asked. "He liked you. He wants to see you again, you know."

Melissa nodded. "He is a nice one." She frowned. "But he doesn't understand the real words either. No one here does."

George glanced over his shoulder at the girl. *You are an odd ducky*, he thought.

A large, midday sun brightened the air and made the ocean glitter as though scaled. They were in a stretch of sand dunes and sea oats and high, wind-driven waves and, except for an occasional lumbering trailer truck, they seemed alone in this world of sleek, eternal forms.

Then Melissa began to cough. The coughing increased in volume, developed a quick, hysterical note.

"Pull over!" Nancy shouted, clutching the child.

George swung the car off the highway and hit the brakes. Gravel pinged against metal, the car fishtailed and lurched to a stop. George was out of the car instantly, in time to catch his daughter and the child in her arms as they came hurtling from the back seat. Melissa's face was red and her small chest heaved. Nancy had her arms around the girl's chest. "Melissa!" Nancy was shouting. "Melissa!"

Nancy jerked the child upwards and back. Melissa's body convulsed. Her breathing was labored, a broken whistle fluttering in her throat.

She shuddered and began to vomit. A hot, green odor, the smell of stagnant tidal pools, assaulted George. Nancy knelt beside Melissa, wiping the child's wet hair from her forehead. "It's gonna be okay, honey," she said. "You got something stuck in your throat. It's all right now. You're all right."

The child jumped up and ran down the beach.

"Melissa!" Nancy screamed, scrambling to her feet and pursuing the girl. George ran after them, fear hissing in him like some power line down in a storm, writhing and spewing sparks.

In her blue dress and knee socks—shoes left behind on the beach now—Melissa splashed into the ocean, arms pumping.

Out of the corner of his eye, George saw Steve come into view. He raced past George, past Nancy, moving with a frenzied pinwheeling of arms. "I got her, I got her, I got her," he chanted.

Don't, George thought. *Please don't.*

The beach was littered with debris, old, ocean-polished bottles, driftwood, seaweed, shattered conch shells. It was a rough ocean, still reverberating to the recent storm.

Steve had almost reached Melissa. George could see him reach out to clutch her shoulder.

Then something rose up in the water. It towered over man and child, and as the ocean fell away from it, it revealed smooth surfaces that glittered and writhed. The world was bathed with light, and George saw it plain. And yet, he could not later recall much detail. It was as though his mind refused entry to this monstrous thing, substituting other images—maggots winking from the eye sockets of some dead animal, flesh growing on a ruined structure of rusted metal—and while, in memory, those images were horrible enough and would not let him sleep, another part of his mind shrank from the knowledge that he had confronted something more hideous and ancient than his reason could acknowledge.

What happened next, happened in an instant. Steve staggered backwards and Melissa turned and ran sideways to the waves.

A greater wave, detached from the logic of the rolling ocean, sped over Steve, engulfing him, and he was gone, while Melissa continued to splash through the tide, now turning and running shoreward. The beast-thing was gone, and the old pattern of waves reasserted itself. Then Steve resurfaced, and with a lurch of understanding, as though the unnatural wave had struck at George's mind and left him dazed, he watched the head bob in the water, roll sickeningly, bounce on the crest of a second wave, and disappear.

Melissa lay face down on the wet sand, and Nancy raced to her, grabbed her up in her arms, and turned to her father.

"Where's Steve?" she shouted over the crash of the surf.

You didn't see then, George thought. *Thank God.*

"Where's Steve?" she shouted again.

George came up to his daughter and embraced her. His touch triggered racking sobs, and he held her tighter, the child Melissa between them.

And what if the boy's head rolls to our feet on the crest of the next wave? George thought, and the thought moved him to action. "Let's get Melissa back to the car," he said, taking the child from his daughter's arms.

It was a painful march back to the car, and George was convinced that at any moment either or both of his charges would bolt. He reached the car and helped his daughter into the back seat. She was shaking violently.

"Hold Melissa," he said, passing the child to her. "Don't let her go, Nancy."

George pulled away from them and closed the car door. He turned then, refusing to look at the ocean as he did so. He looked down, stared for a moment at what was undoubtedly a wet clump of matted seaweed, and knew, with irrational certainty, that Melissa had choked on this same seaweed, had knelt here on the ground and painfully coughed it up.

He told the police that Melissa had run into the waves and that Steve had pursued her and drowned. This was all he could tell them—someday he hoped he would truly believe that it was all there was to tell. Thank god his daughter had not seen. And he realized then, with shame, that it was not even his daughter's feelings that were foremost in his mind but rather the relief, the immense relief, of knowing that what he had seen was not going to be corroborated and that with time and effort, he might really believe it was an illusion, the moment's horror, the tricks light plays with water.

He took the police back to where it had happened. But he would not go down to the tide. He waited in the police car while they walked along the beach.

If they returned with Steve's head, what would he say? *Oh yes, a big wave decapitated Steve. Didn't I mention that? Well, I meant to.*

But they found nothing.

Back at the hotel, George sat at the kitchen table and drank a beer. He was not a drinker, but it seemed to help. "Where's Nancy?" he asked.

"Upstairs," Mrs. Hume said. "She's sleeping with the child. She wouldn't let me take Melissa. I tried to take the child and I thought…I thought my own daughter was going to attack me, hit me. Did she think I would hurt Melissa? What did she think?"

George studied his beer, shook his head sadly to indicate the absence of all conjecture.

Mrs. Hume dried her hands on the dish towel and, ducking her head, removed her apron. "Romner Psychiatric called. A Doctor Melrose."

George looked up. "Is he releasing Mrs. Franklin?" *Please come and get your daughter,* George thought. *I have a daughter of my own.* Oh how he wanted to see the last of them.

"Not just yet. No. But he wanted to know about the family's visits every year. Dr. Melrose thought there might have been something different about that first year. He feels there is some sort of trauma associated with it."

George Hume shrugged. "Nothing out of the ordinary as I recall."

Mrs. Hume put a hand to her cheek. "Oh, but it was different. Don't you remember, George? They came earlier, with all the crowds, and they left abruptly. They had paid for two weeks, but they were gone on the third day. I remember being surprised when they returned the next year—and I thought then that it must have been the crowds they hated and that's why they came so late from then on."

"Well…" Her husband closed his eyes. "I can't say that I actually remember the first time."

His wife shook her head. "What can I expect from a man who can't remember his own wedding anniversary? That Melissa was just a tot back then, a little mite in a red bathing suit. Now that I think of it, she hasn't worn a bathing suit since."

Before going to bed, George stopped at the door to his daughter's room. He pushed the door open carefully and peered in. She slept as she always slept, sprawled on her back, mouth open. She had always fallen asleep abruptly, in disarray, gunned down by the sandman. Tonight she was aided by the doctor's sedatives. The child Melissa snuggled next to her, and for one brief moment the small form seemed sinister and parasitic, as though attached to his daughter, drawing sustenance there.

"Come to bed," his wife said, and George joined her under the covers.

"It's just that she wants to protect the girl," George said. "All she has, you know. She's just seen her boyfriend drown, and this…I think it gives her purpose."

Mrs. Hume understood that this was in answer to the earlier question and she nodded her head. "Yes, I know dear. But is it healthy? I've a bad feeling about it."

"I know," George said.

The shrill ringing of the phone woke him. "Who is it?" his wife was asking as he fumbled in the dark for the receiver.

The night ward clerk was calling from Romner Psychiatric. She apologized for calling at such a late hour, but there might be cause for concern. Better safe than sorry, etc. Mrs. Franklin had apparently—well, had definitely—left the hospital. Should she return to the hotel, the hospital should be notified immediately.

George Hume thanked her, hung up the phone, and got out of bed. He pulled on his trousers, tugged a sweatshirt over his head.

"Where are you going?" his wife called after him.

"I won't be but a minute," he said, closing the door behind him.

The floor was cold, the boards groaning under his bare feet. Slowly, with a certainty born of dread, expecting the empty bed, expecting the worst, he pushed open the door.

Nancy lay sleeping soundly.

The child was gone. Nancy lay as though still sheltering that small, mysterious form.

George pulled his head back and closed the door. He turned and hurried down the hall. He stopped on the stairs, willed his heart to silence, slowed his breathing. "Melissa," he whispered. No answer.

He ran down the stairs. The front doors were wide open. He ran out into the moonlight and down to the beach.

The beach itself was empty and chill; an unrelenting wind blew in from the ocean. The moon shone overhead as though carved from milky ice.

He saw them then, standing far out on the pier, mother and daughter, black shadows against the moon-gray clouds that bloomed on the horizon.

Dear God, George thought. *What does she intend to do?*

"Melissa!" George shouted, and began to run.

He was out of breath when he reached them. Mother and daughter regarded him coolly, having turned to watch his progress down the pier.

"Melissa," George gasped. "Are you all right?"

Melissa was wearing a pink nightgown and holding her mother's hand. It was her mother who spoke: "We are beyond your concern. Mr. Hume. My husband is dead, and without him the contract cannot be renewed."

Mrs. Franklin's eyes were lit with some extraordinary emotion and the wind, rougher and threatening to unbalance them all, made her hair quiver like a dark flame.

"You have your own daughter, Mr. Hume. That is a fine and wonderful thing. You have never watched your daughter die, watched her fade to utter stillness, dying on her back in the sand, sand on her lips, her eyelids; children are so untidy, even dying. It is an unholy and terrible thing to witness."

The pier groaned and a loud crack heralded a sudden tilting of the world. George fell to his knees. A long sliver of wood entered the palm of his hand, and he tried to keep from pitching forward.

Mrs. Franklin, still standing, shouted over the wind. "We came here every year to renew the bargain. Oh, it is not a good bargain. Our daughter is never with us entirely. But you would know, any parent would know, that love will take whatever it can scavenge, any small compromise. Anything less utter and awful than the grave."

There were tears running down Mrs. Franklin's face now, silver tracks. "This year I was greedy. I wanted Melissa back, all of her. And I thought, I am her mother. I have the first claim to her. So I demanded—demanded—that my husband set it all to rights. 'Tell them we have come here for the last year,' I said. And my husband allowed his love for me to override his reason. He did as I asked."

Melissa, who seemed oblivious to her mother's voice, turned away and spoke into the darkness of the waters. Her words were in no language George Hume had ever heard, and they were greeted with a loud, rasping bellow that thrummed in the wood planks of the pier.

Then came the sound of wood splintering, and the pier abruptly tilted. George's hands gathered more spiky wooden needles as he slid forward. He heard himself scream, but the sound was torn away by the renewed force of the wind and a hideous roaring that accompanied the gale.

Looking up, George saw Melissa kneeling at the edge of the pier. Her mother was gone.

"Melissa!" George screamed, stumbling forward. "Don't move,"

But the child was standing up, wobbling, her nightgown flapping behind her.

George leapt forward, caught the child, felt a momentary flare of hope, and then they both were hurtling forward and the pier was gone.

They plummeted toward the ocean, through a blackness defined by an inhuman sound, a sound that must have been the first sound God heard when He woke at the dawn of eternity.

And even as he fell, George felt the child wiggle in his arms. His arms encircled Melissa's waist, felt bare flesh. Had he looked skyward, he would have seen the nightgown, a pink ghost shape, sailing toward the moon.

But George Hume's eyes saw, instead, the waiting ocean and under it, a shape, a moving network of cold, uncanny machinery, and whether it was a living thing of immense size, or a city, or a machine, was irrelevant. He knew only that it was ancient beyond any land-born thing.

Still clutching the child he collided with the hard, cold back of the sea.

George Hume had been raised in close proximity to the ocean. He had learned to swim almost as soon as he had learned to walk. The cold might kill him, would almost certainly kill him if he did not reach shore quickly—but that he did. During the swim toward shore he lost Melissa and in that moment he understood not to turn back, not to seek the child.

He could not tell anyone how he knew a change had been irretrievably wrought and that there was no returning the girl to land. It was not something you could communicate—any more than you could communicate the dreadful ancient quality of the machinery under the sea.

Nonetheless, George knew the moment Melissa was lost to him. It was a precise and memorable moment. It was the moment the child had wriggled, with strange new, sinewy strength, flicked her tail and slid effortlessly from his grasp.

The Oddskeeper's Daughter

*O*ut of the black night, black rain.

Greg sat in the train station and stared grimly out the window at the downpour, his left hand clutching Holly's hologram kiss as though it were the last ticket out of Sweeper City.

Which, actually, it was.

He was going Downtown to decide his fate.

"I see," the clerk had said. "The Numbers took your wife and daughter. You wish to win them back."

The clerk's human aspect was that of a young woman, pleasant-featured, quiet, forgotten in the instant of turning away.

"I am required by law to give you the odds," she had said, her voice shifting to a wire recording. "I am now computing those odds, based on the available data and assuming the information you have presented is accurate." The pause here was for effect, not required. Then: "The odds against winning Holly and Miriam back are 1,230,227 to 1."

Greg nodded again. Slightly better than he had expected, actually.

"I can get you an audience with the Oddskeeper, but, you must understand, it is a final audience."

"Yes."

"All is in order then," she said. "One last formality. I require a statement from you, something motivational."

"Certainly," Greg said. "I am here because I love my wife and daughter more than life itself. My universe makes no sense without them. And…" Greg stared at the flickering, ghost green numbers that scrolled on all the interior walls of all the buildings in Sweeper City.

The pause extended beyond the clerk's listening mode and she uttered a prompt. "Is your statement complete?"

"For the record," Greg said, "I wish to state the obvious. I feel lucky."

They were that unhip, quaint cliché: high school sweethearts. She was in his biology class, three seats up and to his right. He studied the way her cheekbones gathered the sunlight through the window, some strange photosynthesis that created warmth and joy and energy.

Her name was Holly Beale. His name was Greg Halley.

She had come to town in the late fall, six weeks after the beginning of the school year, filling the classroom with her blond suddenness, her blue-eyed smile.

Holly Halley, Greg thought. How could she resist the enticement of such a name? She would have to marry him. He bet his best friend Emmett that he could get her to go to the next dance with him.

"When dogs dance on the moon," Emmett said. Emmett lost five dollars.

"I felt lucky," Greg said when he confessed the bet to Holly.

"Me too," she said, and she kissed him amid the falling leaves, outside the gym, under the star-glazed night. Her sweater crackled with electricity.

Two weeks later she told him she had something to confess.

He nodded, slowly, braced for bad news, a boyfriend in another state, or one closer at hand, or parents moving again, or a sense of physical revulsion in his presence or….

"I'm not human," she said.

He laughed, breathing again, relieved.

"Really," she said. "I'm not kidding."

"It's okay," he said. He was not surprised. It explained her grace, her beauty, her elegance. What young man, deranged by passion, believes his beloved is human? She was an angel, of course.

"No, no angel," she said, laughing, touching his arm.

"Well, what?"

Holly frowned. "That's hard to say. I mean, I know perfectly what I am, but it is hard to explain. I don't know how you would say it. I am someone who could be."

Greg smiled. "Someone who could be."

"Exactly, " Holly said, hugging him. Greg could see she was pleased by his quickness. He hated to disappoint her.

He confessed his confusion.

She tried again. "I guess I belong to a religion. Just as you have religions, the Christian and the Moslem and the Republican and such."

"Well."

"Yes. I am of the religion of events. The miracle of the thing that happens. Because anything that happens is almost impossible. The odds are against it happening when matched with all the things that might have happened in its stead. But it happens, so it is always the miracle, the blind-luck thing."

"I don't follow you," Greg said.

"Kiss me," she said. "I think that will be enough." It was. Happiness is not dependent upon knowing much; love requires no depth of insight into the object of desire. People plummet together in love, often falling for years with nothing but a kiss to steer by.

The question of Holly's humanness did not arise often. In only one way was it truly troubling. She seemed to think she was invulnerable. She had no fear. She would holler and leap from the rocky cliff into the black night waters of the quarry or drive her father's BMW down country roads at unholy speeds while Greg sat next to her, trying not to scream, to prove worthy of this reckless beauty.

Greg's own parents had taught him that fear was an homage to fate. And he was, by nature, cautious, born cautious, prodding his childhood toys with a finger, as though they might contain pins or plastic explosives, taking the first sip of milk with the air of a person suspecting poison.

He was a cautious boy and a cautious young man, and he had fumbled for the condom on the dresser, that first night of their lovemaking when his parents were out of town for the weekend. He had brought Holly to his room after the movie—no guile was required—and they had fallen upon the bed, clothes evaporating, bodies delighted as captured dolphins restored to the sea.

She had snatched the condom from him and tossed it across the room.

It was not a moment for argument, but later Greg expressed his concern. Did she want to get pregnant? They were, after all, still in high school.

Holly had shrugged. It wasn't a matter of wanting, she said. It was her way, the way of her Order. Chance was sacred. You let it be. Only the Evil One fixed the Game. "I am here because I won the lottery of this moment," she said. "Do not dictate to this fate; it is why I am here with you now."

No child had been engendered. Not that time or the times that followed. They moved into their senior year at high school.

"I have never met your parents," Greg said.

"I'll take them out of storage," Holly said. "Although I'm afraid they'll bore you. Their programs are very limited. They are robots, just for show."

So Greg came by on a Saturday night and Holly's mother cooked a pot roast, and Holly's father, who was handsome with silver hair and a square jaw, talked about football.

Holly's parents were a little dull and tended to repeat themselves, but they seemed, to Greg, human enough.

He joked with Holly. "If you have robots for parents, you must be a robot yourself."

Holly rolled her eyes. "Do all people who wear the same suit look alike to you?" she said. "Don't be silly."

She explained. The body of Holly Beale, the bodies of her parents, these mortal, moving husks were authentic. An autopsy would reveal all three bodies to be human in every detail. But two of the bodies were run by limited synaptic overlays. The third, the third was glorious Holly Beale, newly arrived on earth from...another possibility. And if her boyfriend, a lout named Greg, couldn't tell the difference between a couple of glorified toasters and the delightful, world-stopping Holly Beale, then perhaps he didn't deserve her company, perhaps she should seek a more sensitive lover.

Greg apologized for his loutishness. "Don't even tease about leaving me," he said. "I couldn't live without you."

"Careful," Holly said, touching his lips with her finger. "Never threaten the future. Whatever is, is enough."

And now she was gone, and he couldn't let it be enough. He couldn't be satisfied with those years they had spent together.

The rain fell, and he wondered if that was an extension of his mood, of the rain within. When he had come here in the past, with Holly, Sweeper City had been sunny, and the streets had been filled with a festive, noisy crowd.

When you came into Sweeper City from the earthside, it translated humanly. They had come here often, after the child was born. They had placed their small bets, opened their doors, taken their good and their bad and carried it back to Leesburg, Virginia, where they lived.

They had been young and lucky.

Greg boarded the train, found an empty seat. He would have preferred his own company, but the car quickly became crowded, and a middle-aged man with wire-rimmed glasses and a bowler hat sat next to him.

"Mind if I smoke?" the man asked, producing a pipe.

"Not at all."

The man stared at the glowing hologram in Greg's hand. "Petition?" he asked.

"Yes."

"Sweetheart?"

"My wife."

The man nodded and sucked reflectively on his pipe. He sighed. "Random we come, Random we go," he said.

It was a harmless statement. Any denizen of Sweeper City might have uttered it. It produced, in Greg, an irrational rage, and he wanted to put his hands around this complacent facsimile's neck and strangle it, screaming all the while, "Your luck ran out. You sat next to an infidel." Instead, Greg stared out the window as the lights of Sweeper City rolled out and away and the darkness of the countryside turned the window into a black mirror. He regarded himself, an intense young man with dark hair, a melancholy aspect, and an unsettling look of resignation in his eyes, as though he had already accepted defeat, had seen the scrolling sea of numbers suddenly stop and turn red, a failed match from which there was no appeal.

The voice would boom from the black ceiling: "She is dead forever and so is the child. It is what it is. This petition has been duly executed, and no more appeals may be presented. The petitioner will await the judgment of the Oddskeeper."

That judgment would be death, another tide of numbers that would drown him in their indifference. And his extinction would be a footnote, an inconsequential thing. He would already be dead, killed when the last door of possibility shut, when Holly and Miriam were gone forever and meaning was leached from his life.

They graduated from high school. They had both applied and been accepted at the University of Virginia and that is where they went. Friends of either were always surprised that the two did not room together for they seemed to live in an intensely private world of lovers' signals. In the company of others they were polite but distant, incapable of hiding the truth: that the world beyond their mutual delight was a chimera filled with wraiths, faint voices, and vague social protocols.

"We'll live together when we are married," Holly told Greg. "I've got to break the news to my father."

"I thought your father was a robot?"

Holly frowned, not amused. "My *real* father. You haven't met him yet. He won't approve of you. He wouldn't approve of anyone. He thinks the more attachments one has, the more the odds go against one."

"Great philosophy," Greg said.

Holly kissed Greg on the lips. "He'll come around," she said. "He dotes on me."

They married the year they received their undergraduate degrees. The wedding was small, some friends from the University, Greg's parents and sister, Holly's robot parents.

"I see your father didn't make it," Greg said. "Your *real* father."

"No," Holly said, suddenly sad. "He has accepted our marriage, but it is painful for him."

On the night before the marriage, Holly invited Greg over to her garage apartment. More often, she would spend the night in the duplex he rented near the University. Holly said, "You have never asked where I go."

"No," Greg said, and the flutter of his heart told him why. He was afraid the knowledge might somehow tear them apart. Those times when she was absent, when he would drive by her apartment and see her car out front but no one home, when peering through the windows would reveal empty, lighted rooms…He wasn't sure he wanted to know where she went.

She seemed to sense this, and she drew him closer. "I do not go far, really," she said. "And you are in my thoughts wherever I am. But we are to be married. You need to see my home. It will be the arena of our dreams."

She took him to Sweeper City. That night the doorway was located under the bed. More often, it frequented the closet. Once Greg learned the trick of seeing it, he would sometimes see it in actual motion, skulking along a baseboard or, on summer days, lying in the bathtub like a cat seeking refuge from the heat.

"This unlocks the door," she said, and she showed him the glowing hologram, and he recognized her lips immediately, slightly parted, bright red and luminous. "A kiss." A kiss locked in a ruby the size of a baseball. To create your hologram, you leaned forward, you kissed the key-making machine, kissed the shiny, crystal surface. Pretended, perhaps, that it was your heart's desire.

Lips kissing lips. The hologram forged in this kiss could open the door. On the other side, image acknowledged image.

"This is your key," she said. "Should you ever need to go alone, you will need this for the coming and going."

Sweeper City. Where was it really? All the answers were unsatisfactory, meaningless, irrelevant. It was in an unimaginably distant future. It was a parallel universe. It was the home of the human-bodied entity called now Holly Halley and it was the home of all her kind. Or, more precisely according to Holly, it could have been her home. It was the possibility of such a place. It was Holly's dream had she existed to dream it.

Sweeper City was a religion or perhaps the artifact of a religion or—

Greg told his beloved that she had answered the question in sufficient detail for the present. He took her hand and held it tightly as they walked through the city, which was something of a cross between Las Vegas and Disney World.

"That's human seeing," Holly said, and he didn't ask her to explain it.

The streets were thronged with people, balloons in the air, confetti at their feet, a clown hoisting a trumpet to his lips and making a rude, raucous noise.

"Come on," Holly said. She led him into a casino called *Tumbling Dice*.

At the roulette wheel that night, they won Holly's pregnancy and, in a side bet, her job at a local ad agency.

Greg was exhausted that night. and he could not sleep upon his return from the city. He was unhappy with the knowledge that his life was governed by games of chance.

Holly's voice was a soft breeze on his naked shoulders, full of warmth and explaining, a litany of explaining. "The present is the sum of all the accidents before it. Every day is more improbable than the last, since the path is longer, the twisting greater."

"I like to think I have some measure of free will," Greg complained. He felt as though his lover had somehow tricked him, that while he labored at his studies, she played cards to secure him a passing grade.

"There is nothing freer than the fall of the Numbers,"

Holly said. "And your will is there. Sweeper City is created in your eyes; it must obey your understanding of the natural way. I don't know why you have to get so upset. You have to admit I'm a pretty good gambler. We haven't had to go Downtown, have we? Not once."

"Downtown?" Greg had rolled over to face her. He offered a long, appraising stare

"Well," Holly said, "Downtown. Yes...."

"Tell me about Downtown. I don't like the sound of Downtown."

He was right not to like it. After some prodding, Holly explained that Downtown was where the big gambles were resolved. In the Hall of the Oddskeeper. While the Sisters of the Wheel looked on, their cold, sunken eyes hidden in the shadows of their hooded robes.

The train slowed, a low rumbling. The lights of the tunnel flicked by at regular intervals, light beats. The man with the pipe stood up. "Well," he said, "may your Numbers bring you Harmony."

"Thank you," Greg said. He watched the man push through the crowded car.

Greg waited until the car cleared before standing and moving down the aisle himself. Stepping down from the car into the chill, echoing vault of the station, images assaulted him. He saw, in an instant, Holly, stumbling, reaching out with a hand to steady herself against the wall, saying, "I'm all right," and pushing herself away from the wall and moving forward again, saying, "I just want to go home," and imprinted on the yellow wall, imprinted on Greg's mind, the bright red stain of her palm.

The underground station was daunting; great slabs of stone the color of wet cement rose up into darkness. Greg had forgotten none of it. Fear would have flattened him now, pushed reason from his mind, and he would have begun screaming, running across the shiny black floor in the inexplicable desolation—where had the crowded train's passengers gone?—but he raged against the fear. Anger kept him sane.

How could her own father have let it happen?

Charmed lives. They named their daughter Miriam. After Greg got his master's in engineering, they moved to Leesburg, Virginia, where a job awaited him, working for a firm in Fairfax, a thirty-minute commute in the morning. His fellow workers were intelligent and friendly. The work was engaging. His love for his wife and daughter seemed boundless.

When his daughter was five, she fell out of a tree and broke her arm. Holly called Greg at work. He met her at the hospital.

When he entered the room where his daughter lay unconscious, Greg felt his heart give a small, sharp twist, as though pierced by a scalpel. He knelt by her bed and touched her cheek. A white plaster cast, bent slightly and running the full length of her arm, was hoisted in the air by wires connected to a gleaming steel rod.

"She will be all right," Holly said.

That is what the doctors had said, but that this could happen at all terrified Greg. In the company of his fearless wife, he had forgotten the fundamental hostility of an indifferent world. He had ignored all the minefields of mortality. He had forsaken his own religion, a religion of dread, of the certainty of dangerous, malign, stalking forces. He felt guilty now, sick with the sense that his complacency had allowed the accident to occur. If he had been properly vigilant, his daughter would not have suffered.

Holly tried to comfort him. She failed. When Miriam came home from the hospital, she was still in pain. He would hear her crying and go in and talk to her, and she would fall asleep, but he would remain awake all night.

His wife saw his pain. One night, a week after their daughter had come home from the hospital, she said, "We can appeal. I did not want to bring it up, because the odds are long. But we can appeal."

He did not understand, at first, what she was saying. And later, when he thought he understood, he still failed to comprehend. Perhaps he heard only what was necessary for hope. Perhaps she mentioned consequences, and he chose not to hear those words.

He heard only that Miriam might not have to suffer. He heard that events were not unalterable. What the Numbers had allowed, the Numbers could revoke. In the hall of the Oddskeeper, amid the falling Numbers, Holly could challenge the randomness of events, and if luck were on her side, the new order would take precedence. It would be as though Miriam had never climbed that tree, never tumbled, never hit the ground so rudely.

"Why didn't you say this before?" Greg asked.

And perhaps she answered then. If so, he did not hear.

They rode the train Downtown. They sat in the great antechamber and waited for the Sisters of the Wheel to come.

"Which is the Gameplayer?" the robed woman asked.

"I am," Holly said. She was taken away. And Greg waited, observing his fellow petitioners, all of whom were still and silent, dark, hunched figures that hugged themselves to keep from flying apart, waiting in purgatory for the dice to roll.

The morning wore into afternoon. The elderly woman returned, threw back her hood, looked coolly into Greg's eyes. She possessed grey eyes, the translucent grey of an overcast sky, cold-weather eyes. For one disorienting moment, Greg thought he confronted his wife's solemn features, aged suddenly by adversity. Then the woman spoke, breaking the spell. "I am sorry. The Numbers were not with your wife today. If you will follow me."

She lay on a hospital bed in a small cubicle. In the next cubicle, someone was moaning. Greg couldn't tell if the sufferer were man or woman; pain and grief overrode gender.

Holly's eyes opened. "I'm all right," she said.

Her left hand was bandaged.

"What happened?" he asked.

She smiled wanly. Her face was very pale. She lifted her right hand and touched his cheek. "The Numbers weren't with me," she said. "It' s okay."

"What happened to your hand?" There were tears in her eyes. She pushed herself upright, using her right hand against the mattress. She was wearing a gray hospital gown.

"I want to get out of here," she said. "I want you to help me get dressed, and I want to get out of here."

He had helped her dress. She had balanced against him. He felt her body tremble as she gripped his shoulder. Once her bandaged hand bumped the bed railing as she struggled into her shirt. She cried out.

Helping her through the station, he caught her when she stumbled. The gauze bandage had come unraveled, and her hand against the wall left a bloody print. He knelt beside her and rewrapped the hand, shaken, filled with vertiginous terror. He saw where the ring and little finger had been severed, large black stitches like a row of black flies.

"I'm sorry," he said, and the inadequacy of the words threatened to burn away his reason.

Later, much later, he said, "What kind of creature is this Oddskeeper? What sort of monster?"

"He is no monster," Holly said. "He is my father. I know it grieved him greatly, but it is the Way of the Wheel. The Numbers spoke against me. I paid the wager. I would have been disgraced if it were otherwise. Besides, happiness is not lodged in a few fingers of the left hand."

She kissed him then.

His daughter's broken arm mended. Once again she raced through the perilous world as though invulnerable.

Five years of good luck followed. In retrospect: five years of *uncommonly* good luck. They had lived a charmed life. Did he ever stop to question it? What about those promotions? He had worked hard; he deserved them. But did it ever occur to him that good things did not inevitably follow on the heels of merit and hard work?

Had he felt lucky? Truthfully, he had not. Living inside one's luck, one comes to expect the good thing.

Their bets in Sweeper City had been small, the minimum required by Holly's world.

Holly would urge him to take bigger risks. "It is the Longer Odds that accrue the greater Honor," she would say.

"We are doing all right, aren't we?" he would say.

She did not dispute that, and the strange, solemn, and fearful shadows that momentarily clouded her eyes were, Greg thought, her warring demons, marshaled through love and her husband's better judgment.

She must have suspected all along.

Once she even voiced it. "I'm scared," she said. "I mean, everyone has to go Downtown sometime. We haven't had to. Not once."

He remembered the night she said it. They were preparing for bed. She had just showered, and stood before him naked, drying her wet hair with a towel, her eyes staring wistfully at the wall as though ghost numbers swarmed before her eyes.

That day, they had won twenty-five thousand dollars in the statewide lottery. A day for rejoicing, surely. The sum would allow them to buy the house, the perfect house, the house they had walked through for the tenth time the previous day knowing it was just out of their reach.

"To win such a thing," she said, "we should have had to go Downtown. Although, I don't really know. Perhaps there is a luck here all its own."

She spoke to reassure herself. "Everything is improbable,"

she said. "There is no reason that this improbability cannot be. It is what it is."

He smiled at his wife's distraction and urged her to come to bed. He stretched out his arms and she came to him, returning his smile.

"The most amazing, improbable thing in the entire universe," he said, "is you in my arms."

She giggled then, hugged him tightly. He sensed her acceptance, manifested in a sudden fierce sensuality, and he followed her into the irrefutable logic of their intertwining.

What could they have done then? In truth, nothing. The die had already been cast or, more dreadfully, the die had not been cast at all.

Now he sat on the cold bench in the antechamber of the Hall of the Oddskeeper. His fellow petitioners were few. The room seemed bigger than he remembered it, but he was coming here alone this time. The world was vast and hostile now.

The robed woman came for him. Her face was in shadow. He thought she might be the same woman who had led Holly away when they sought to avert their daughter's fall from a tree. But then, perhaps all the Sisters of the Wheel spoke with the same clipped authority and strode across marble floors with the same imperial bearing. They were all familiar, one person he had known.

Greg followed her down the hall. The door opened and he entered the room that would decide his fate. Holly had spoken of it only once, and then briefly, but he recognized it instantly. A green, underwater sea of numbers flowed on all the walls. The Sisters of the Wheel led him to the dark, stone chair and the Oddskeeper mounted the steps and stood before him and spoke.

"It is what it is," the Oddskeeper said. "It will be what it will be."

The figure was robed and dark against the waterfall of numbers behind him. But the voice was unmistakable. Greg had been afraid a different man might serve.

This was the one. This was the voice he knew, the terrible messenger from that terrible day.

Perhaps luck was still with him, a bitter, poisonous luck, the luck of lost souls.

Two weeks ago. Another country. He had been running late at the office, and he called Holly. She was not there, and he spoke into the answering machine. "See if you can get Beth to watch Miriam tonight. I'll be home before seven, and I've got some news that requires a fancy restaurant for the telling. See you."

The bonus was utterly unexpected. Five thousand out-of-nowhere dollars.

Holly's car was not in the driveway. The phone was ringing as he unlocked the door.

The answering phone message began to play, and he snatched up the phone, shutting it off.

"Mr. Greg Halley?"

He would have denied it, if that would have helped. He recognized the official voice immediately, the grim, end-of-the-line voice, the voice that identified itself as an officer with the Fairfax County Police Department.

When he hung up the phone, Miriam and Holly were dead, killed in a car accident. The accident involved no other cars. Beyond that, he knew nothing. The horror left no room for details.

He turned and walked upstairs and into the bedroom.

An old man was sitting on the bed. He wore a monk's robe. The hood was thrown back to reveal a large, rough-hewn head, grey hair flaring like a lion's mane, a great, corrugated forehead, blue, weary eyes.

He looked up at Greg.

"You would be Holly's husband," he said.

"Who are you?" But, of course, Greg knew who it was. The question was really "Why?" or "How could this happen?"

The Oddskeeper stood up. "I have lost a daughter and a granddaughter. You have lost a wife and a daughter. We are one in our tragedy,"

"We are not one," Greg said, the anger flaring. He remembered his wife's severed fingers.

"You are right to hate me," the Oddskeeper said. "But you hate in ignorance, and I would prefer you hate in knowledge. Informed hatred has a cleaner edge."

The Oddskeeper explained.

His daughter had sought the human way. An indulgent parent, he had let her enter that universe. She had married there, taken hostages to fortune. He had watched her progress with misgivings.

She had done well. The Numbers seemed to love her. She gambled with a clear mind and a proud heart, and she prospered.

Then, foolishly, she wished to argue the judgment brought against her daughter. She wished to revoke an accident which was, all things considered, minor.

And she lost.

"I watched the Counterdown take her fingers," the old man said, his voice revisiting that place of pain. He had seen such things before, of course, far harsher consequences. But this was his daughter, and her pain was multiplied within him.

"I was devastated. 'It is what it is,' I said, but I had lost my faith and saw another way. I resolved that my daughter would not be harmed again. I put her above the Numbers. I sinned. I manipulated the outcome. I defied Chance. I turned my back on Randomness and the Kingdom."

"Then why—"

"I grew greedy of good fortune. Proud. I wanted to protect my daughter, to spare her pain. But I went further than that. Like a doting god, I showered her with gifts. I went too far. It seems the Council has suspected me for some time. Today they found me in the Matrix engineering another miracle, your—how do you say it?—*bonus*. As you would say in this world, they caught me with my red hands."

Greg leaned over and clutched the old man's shoulders. "And they performed this horror? They killed Holly and Miriam to punish *you*?"

The old man shook his head sadly. "There is no *punish* in our world. The cause and effect of *punish* is foreign to us. They merely stopped my meddling. They shut down the long run of fortuitous events. The inevitable balance was restored."

The old man pushed Greg's arms from his shoulders and rose. He was taller than Greg and spoke with new-summoned dignity. "You are right to hate me. My solicitude created the vacuum into which this tragedy rushed. It is my doing. I cannot undo it. I am dead, felled by the accident of my pride. I go on because I have no choice."

He brushed past Greg and flung the closet door open. He turned. "I am sorry, my son. I am done with your world now, and you are done with mine. We have nothing but sorrow between us. Goodbye."

When Greg rushed to the closet, the Oddskeeper was gone. The doorway to Sweeper City narrowed. Shrinking to the size of a ruler, it slid to the floor and darted past Greg and under the bed. When Greg pushed the bed away, he found nothing but dust and a single dirty sweat sock.

"I have an appeal!" he screamed. "I am entitled to an appeal!"

The ears that might have heard such an appeal were far away, perhaps had never existed.

He attended the funeral with his parents. Their faces showed him his own, pale, misshapen by grief. They had loved Holly and Miriam. The smallness of his daughter's coffin was blinding, a blasphemy that demanded the world be torn apart.

He quit his job. He withdrew all his savings and went to Las Vegas. He lost all the money he had, lost it with a disinterest that attracted women. A sharp-faced woman with the smile of a carnivore asked him if he would like to come up to her room.

"I'm sorry," he said. "I'm a married man."

He went back to his hotel room late at night and lay down fully clothed. He could not sleep, and he snapped the table lamp on and stared at the ceiling. He had a prize-winning headache; the shadows on the walls seemed to skitter like cockroaches. He got up and fished in his suitcase. He brought the bright red globe of Holly's hologram kiss back to the bed and cradled it on his stomach.

"I've gambled it all," he muttered. "I've played by the rules. So."

He waited. He decided it would not come.

And then it came. It slid from under the bathroom door and expanded on the floor in front of him.

He dived from the bed, falling into Sweeper City with a shout of savage triumph.

Now he sat in the chair, in the Hall of the Oddskeeper, prepared for the final game. The odds were 1,230,227 to 1 against him.

"Greg Halley," the Oddskeeper intoned. "You are bound, in this appeal, to accept the decision of the Numbers. If the fall of the Numbers does not match your keyed decision, you will accept the judgment of this Hall. If Randomness invokes your side of the argument, your wife and daughter will be restored to pre-catastrophic event status and you will be free to leave and find your fate in the common lot of your kind."

"Father," Greg shouted, "my number is 9382."

"I am not your father," the Oddskeeper said, "and you are to key the number in on the panel in front of you. Your oral recitation is not required."

"You are my father-in-law," Greg said. "We both loved Holly and Miriam."

The Oddskeeper nodded. "Yes. I grieve for us all."

"One other grieves."

"Who would that be?"

"Holly's mother."

The Oddskeeper shook his head. "You have made a human analogy that does not, I fear, apply. Holly has no mother; I am her sole progenitor."

"I'm sorry," Greg said. "But that is not possible. Not humanly. And I am here from the human side."

"And who would this human-Conjured mother be?"

"Surely a Sister of the Wheel. Who else?"

I have seen her, Greg thought. *I have seen her guiding Holly into this room.*

"I am afraid your human imaging does not have that sort of power here. I must ask you to key in your number."

"How many are the Sisters of the Wheel?"

"They number eight."

"I count seven in this room."

The Oddskeeper paused, his eyes traveling the room. He saw the seven, too, but said, "Your Number."

Greg slowly punched the keys. 9, 3, 8, 2.

The walls scrolled, blinking savagely.

I've lost.

The walls turned red. "No match," the Oddskeeper said.

The eighth Sister entered the room, walking briskly across the floor.

"Wait," she said. "I believe we have an interface malfunction. I will retype the petitioner's number."

"There is no precedent for this," the Oddskeeper shouted.

The room was still as the Sister threw back her hood and

stared up toward the man at the top of the stairs.

"Your heart," she said. "And what you remember. That is precedent enough."

She looked down, the hood falling back, recalling her face to shadows. She typed the number.

The walls blinked, went blank, then swarmed again with numbers. A blaze of yellow filled the room.

"A match," the Oddskeeper said. "The Numbers have recognized your appeal."

The Oddskeeper followed Greg into the antechamber. "When you return, Holly and Miriam will be there. The event is eradicated. Your life from here on will progress according to the fortunes of your world."

"Thank you," Greg said.

"You do not understand the gravity of what you have done. You have, in your words, damned us all. There is not a person in that room who did not witness the gravest sin our culture can know."

Greg waited, silent, feeling the old man's weariness and loss.

"We watched the Numbers fall to tampering, to base Will, to a mother's love."

Greg put a hand on his father-in-law's shoulder. "There is a higher law," he said.

"None higher than the Numbers."

"Holly told me that the greater odds outweigh the lesser odds, that this is always so in any situation and determines the final outcome in your trials."

"Yes. This is so."

"Ask your machines for the odds that I would find Holly in my universe and love her fiercely and conjure up that love in others and subvert the Sisters of the Wheel and cloud the judgment of the Oddskeeper himself. Ask for those odds."

Something like comprehension came into the Oddskeeper's eyes. Greg turned away and walked toward the doorway, Holly's ruby kiss burning his palm.

He heard the old man mutter behind him. "We have kept faith," he whispered. "We *have* kept faith."

On her seventeenth birthday, Miriam Halley kissed a young man named James Markham.

"I am the luckiest man in the world," he told her.

"That's true," she said, repeating her father's words, "as long as you don't forget it."

The Death
of the Novel

*T*he lecture was going well, and then the young man stood up. He was dressed in black, an unfortunate fashion that had resurfaced—with black shirts supplanting turtlenecks. His face was as white as soap except for a line of acne that stitched across his forehead, suggesting bullet wounds. He said what he had come to say and left. Latham, renowned for his calm, his unflappable demeanor, continued his lecture.

"There's only one plot," Latham told his students. "Hero encounters adversity. Hero triumphs or fails." Latham paused. When one gave lectures to the young, one learned to speak with some authority. College sophomores were not interested in subtleties. Give them a good, flamboyant dose of absolutes and they listened. He had been teaching the same creative writing class for fifteen years now, and he had distilled the opinions of a lifetime into stark one-liners, opinions as hefty as facts.

"Plot," Professor Ron Latham said, loosening his tie and walking to the open window, "is what God forgot. The artist has an obligation to remedy that oversight." Latham looked out the window. It had rained earlier in the day, and the sun was now beating on the asphalt parking lot. A group of students leaned against a car, talking, laughing. A green breeze blew through the classroom, urging truancy. He turned away from the window and nodded to the girl whose hand was raised. She stood up.

"It seems to me," she said, "that a story should be spontaneous, should just happen while you are writing it. Like life. Organically. Plot is artificial, dead."

Latham smiled. The girl had short, blond hair and exquisite eyebrows. Samantha Clark. Her classmates called her Sam. He thought of saying, "I concede to the beauty of your eyebrows, Sam. The profundity of your blue eyes blows to irrelevant bits any arguments I might offer." But he did not. He would wait and say it to her later, if the opportunity arose—and, more often than not, it did.

"Miss Clark," he said, "there are many who would agree with you. Plot is a convenience, like our skeletons. Our skeletons are handy things to hang our flesh on, don't you think? Otherwise we'd have to slide around. I'll grant you there is a lot of boneless fiction in the world, but that doesn't mean that we are obligated to create more."

The class laughed. The discussion of plot continued, and by the time the class ended, some of the heat of the young man's outburst had been diffused. The room emptied quickly. Latham sat at his desk and studied the class log. Brackenridge. There was the name, all right. Dorian Brackenridge. Such a Gothic name. But this was the first time the boy had ever attended a class. Latham was sure of that. Well. So Lisa Brackenridge had a brother. Was there a resemblance? Something in the mouth, perhaps, a petulant fullness? But she had never spoken of a brother. Had she? A man could not remember everything that was whispered in his ear. Latham seemed to remember something about a sister, but no brother. So, a brother.

And the brother had stood in Latham's class, shaking visibly, and said, "How about this for a story? Lecherous college professor seduces young innocent gullible student, who doesn't understand what an old and cynical game it is. She is abandoned, learns that she is one of many, and in despair she takes her life. Is that the stuff of fiction or does it lack sufficient plot? Or is my sister's death simply a cliché, Dr. Latham?"

These were not the sort of questions you responded to, and the young man hadn't waited for a reply in any event. He had ended on a sob of anguish and bolted from the room. There was no truth to what he said, of course. Latham had had a brief affair, two years ago, with Lisa Brackenridge, a quiet student whose round features and average looks were redeemed by large, dark eyes, a wonderfully compact body, and an ardent, breathless devotion. But the affair had been over for some months before she took her life. And, indeed, she had accepted the end of the affair quietly. Her exact words...well he couldn't remember her exact words, but they were reasonable words. She understood, wished him well, etc.

Latham gathered the manuscripts that students had left on his desk, swept them into his briefcase, and left the room.

Walking briskly, he breathed in the muddy, honeysuckle air of April. Off in the distance, at the bottom of the library's steps, a black-clad figure was being embraced by a blond girl, and as Latham rounded a corner and lost them to view the curious notion that young Samantha was locked in the arms of Dorian Brackenridge presented itself. A curious notion, indeed, and one he instantly dismissed, reflecting that as his eyesight diminished his imagination increased.

That Dorian Brackenridge had unsettled Latham was a fact, but Latham was fully recovered now. The intensity of youth was unsettling—such a stew of hormones! A middle-aged man could swim in all that emotional excitement, but he couldn't partake of it. Latham loved being around it, felt it like the wind from a passing freight train, this wild turbulence of youth, but he wasn't in danger of being hit by the train. They failed exams and leapt off buildings. They yelled themselves hoarse at football games and wept if they lost. They fell in love as though betting their souls. How bracing to be around them! There were far worse lots in life than being an English teacher noted for eccentricity in a small North Carolina college. If he was a bit of a fraud, with his tweed jackets and the pipe he didn't smoke and his careful air of dishevelment, well, everyone was a little bit of a phony. Society demanded it.

Something rattled under his foot, sliding along the concrete walk. He bent down and retrieved what proved to be a five-sided locket of gold on a gold chain. Standing on the sidewalk, he tried to open it, but either the spring was broken or he was going about it wrong. He slipped it into the pocket of his jacket, resolving to drop it off at the student union where lost objects were routinely taken.

That night, having flipped through half a dozen student stories, at least three of which were bleaker than anything Celine or Camus had ever contrived, Latham picked up a manuscript typed on yellow legal paper. The typewriter could have used a new ribbon and the characters were not aligned; the word "NOVEL," for instance, contained an "0" that jumped from the heart of the word and an "E" that slumped drunkenly against the "L."

At the top of the first page was typed, in all caps: THE DEATH OF THE NOVEL. No author's name followed, but this wasn't unusual. Over the years, a number of his students had submitted anonymous manuscripts. If their teacher hailed the story as a work of genius, they could come forward. If not, they could sulk in the shadows, at least free of public humiliation. The author would almost always give himself (or herself) away during a reading of the manuscript. The pain of authorship was a hard thing to hide.

Latham settled into the armchair, poured himself a small glass of brandy, and read:

I wish I had the imagination to tell a story but
I don't. I don't think I have any imagination at all.

I know I don't dream. I used to dream when my sister was alive, but her death robbed me of all that.

Latham sighed. Guess we know who wrote this, he thought. He gave a mental shrug and continued reading.

Having no story to tell, none of my own, I have taken my father's runes, although forbidden, and rattled them in my father's skull and called on various Forms and sustained such wounds as they gave and so, at last, the Howling One has answered and said it is done and so it is done. There is no fork in the road, no deliverance, no other journey now.

Here the author had skipped a couple of lines and, in all caps, typed: CHAPTER ONE. Then:

She had on her person a small tattoo of a pentagram, and within the pentagram two serpents guarded a dove. It was a tattoo of protection, given her by her father, but it could not save her from the man, because he was not himself evil but only capable of doing great evil, and she was in love and so unprotected, for love is welcoming and defenseless.

Latham stopped reading. They had been lying in bed when he had noticed her tattoo. He hadn't noticed it the first few times they had made love. It had been dark; she had been shy. The tattoo was the size of a quarter and it was on her back. "My heart beats above it," she said. He asked her about it, but she shrugged. "I was a real headbanger in my youth. Did lots of drugs, shaved off all my hair. Father was quite worried about me. Tattoos were the least of it."

He hadn't questioned her again. He was not a curious man. He read on.

> The first time they made love, he was impotent, having drunk too much, and this weakness won her heart. She was bound to him after that and so he had the power to kill her.

"Jesus," Latham said, dropping the yellow page to the floor. Lisa must have sent an in-depth account back to her brother—her *brother* for Christ's sake! Latham shook his head. He sure as hell wasn't going to read this stuff in class. Although the writing wasn't bad...

He read on. The account was detailed and occasionally embarrassing. There was a fairly devastating physical description of the professor that was more than a little cruel—sure, he was a few pounds overweight, but he didn't actually quiver when he walked. And the conversations...they jogged memories, but surely he hadn't spoken so condescendingly, so pompously.

Chapter one ended with spring break and Lisa leaving for Boston, her home, and the professor casting his eye about and discovering a redheaded cheerleader who couldn't hear enough about Chaucer. Melanie. Had her name really been Melanie? Latham couldn't remember. There was no chapter two that night, but in the days and weeks that followed, the chapters materialized. Although Dorian Brackenridge did not make another appearance in class, the chapters duly made their way to Latham's desk. They were there after class. Latham made some effort to discover who was putting them there, but he gave up. They were no longer on the telltale yellow paper—in fact the paper varied each time and there were plenty of students tossing manuscripts on his desk. The chapters were typed on the same typewriter, however. Latham was by now familiar with its wobbly typeface.

The chapters were unpleasant reading, but he could not help himself. They were strangely dramatic and engrossing. He might have been reading about a stranger. And he was; he was. He had never been that callous, that calculating, had he? In chapter fourteen she killed herself—alone in a dorm room—and Latham was sick with remorse. She had taken a butcher's knife to her throat, an act of great determination and desperation, forcing the blade under the jaw, beneath the ear. Had he had any critical faculties left, Latham might have admired the writing, as cold as ice yet passionate. But he had lost all enthusiasm for craft.

He was a haunted man, and he fell into Samantha Clark's arms seeking refuge. He needed the girl, her blond, blazing, blue-eyed lust and her utter lack of morbidity, to save him from himself and the darkness that was closing in on him. She should have been an easy conquest. From the first afternoon meeting, held ostensibly to discuss a story she was working on, it was clear that she was willing. The way she touched his shoulder with her hand, the way her voice would suddenly lower as she leaned forward…these were clear signals. But he hesitated, feeling, for the first time in years, a cold self-doubt.

Awkwardly, and with a grim resolve that had little to do with lust, he took her to bed. The affair, once begun, proved efficacious. The gloom was dispelled. He was able to breathe again. He looked around and saw that it was late May, the world in a riot of renewal. And the chapters ceased arriving. Perhaps the death scene was the last of them.

"Your eyes are the blue that the ocean dreams of when it dreams of the sky." Latham told her.

"You say that to all the girls," Sam said, giggling and dancing out of bed toward the bathroom.

"Only to the blue-eyed ones," he shouted after her.

He heard the shower hiss and tossed on a robe and walked out onto the porch where he retrieved the paper from under the porch swing. A garish headline greeted him: STUDENT KILLED IN RITUAL MURDER. There was a picture of Brackenridge, only his name wasn't Brackenridge, it was Jameson and he was an acting student at the nearby community college and somebody had killed him. His body had been mutilated and certain organs had been removed. The newspaper refrained from saying which organs were taken, but Latham, no stranger to the times, thought: *His heart. They took his heart.*

Latham read the article twice. Jameson had a mother and father in Atlanta. He was an only child.

"You okay?" Sam asked, brushing her hair.

That night Latham found chapter fifteen among the student manuscripts he had taken home for the weekend. He lay in bed and read it. Chapter fifteen ended like this:

> On his way home, the professor found a gold
> locket. Failing in his attempts to pry it open, he
> put it in his pocket and forgot about it.

Latham had forgotten about the locket. Was it still there? How did the author know about the locket? Latham got out of bed and began rummaging through the pockets of his jackets, and when he touched the cold metal, he jumped back as though bitten. Holding the chain between thumb and forefinger, he watched the golden pentagon revolve before his eyes.

Sitting up in bed, he placed it on his open palm. He touched it and it opened slowly to reveal a small, five-sided piece of parchment, two serpents guarding a dove, and then, with a conviction that filled him with revulsion, that sent him leaping from the bed as he hurled the locket and its contents across the room, he realized that this was no parchment facsimile and that Lisa Brackenridge, wherever she lay, was missing a stamp-sized piece of her skin.

Later, when he had ceased shaking and conquered his revulsion, he crawled around on the floor seeking the locket and its grisly contents. He found the locket, but the scrap of tattooed skin was gone, not under the bed or the dresser. Gone. He couldn't sleep that night and canceled classes the next morning. He found Sam's address in his wallet and drove over to the garage apartment where she lived. He had never been there before; never, on principle, did he visit the dwellings of any of his young lovers. He climbed the steps to her apartment and knocked. There was no answer and he knocked again, finally trying the doorknob which turned in his hand.

The room contained a single bed, a dresser, a desk upon which an old, hump-backed typewriter sat, and a chair. The room felt vacant, deserted, less home than a motel room, and Latham could not envision the vital, athletic Sam inhabiting such a room. He sat in the chair, unable to think clearly, waiting. He got up, looked in the closet, and found it empty. That sent him to the dresser drawers, also empty. Now he waited for her return, but would she return at all, had she gone for good? A fist seemed to close over his heart, a new sensation of regret and terrible yearning. The room grew dark in the dusk and he turned on the overhead light. He would leave her a note. He picked up a sheet of paper and typed: SAM— PLEASE COME BY WHEN YOU GET THIS NOTE. I WAITED ALL DAY FOR YOU. —RON. The letters wobbled on the page. He had expected as much. It was as though he were writing chapter sixteen himself. Lisa had had a sister, not a brother.

Again he was not surprised when, returning home, he found chapter sixteen waiting for him on the end table next to the sofa. It began:

> That night the professor heard a rustling
> noise that seemed to come from behind the

chest of drawers. In the dark, the sound formed an image in his mind. He envisioned a large moth trapped between the chest of drawers and the wall, beating its wings into ragged tatters as it climbed the wall and then fell back, gathering dust. Only it was not a moth, but something else entirely, something growing in the darkness, something driven by love.

Latham put the manuscript down. He was under no obligation to read it. He did not have to read it if he chose not to. He chose not to.

That night he heard the beating of small wings and lay in sweating terror until, at last, the sound died. And then he jumped from bed, turned all the lights on, pushed the dresser from the wall, and searched the room. He found nothing. All day he resisted the temptation to read any more of the chapter. He slept some that night, fitfully, but felt no sense of relief with the dawn. On his doorstep, under the newspaper, he found chapter seventeen. He sat on the sofa in his underwear and read the rest of chapter sixteen and all of chapter seventeen.

He dialed Sam's number and a recording told him the number was no longer in operation. He drove by her apartment, and this time the door was locked. As he was coming down the stairs an elderly woman shouted to him: "If you are looking for Miss Clark she's moved back to Boston. Said to tell anyone who came by that her sister would attend to her affairs. That's the way she said it: 'attend to her affairs.'"

Latham returned to his house and reread chapters sixteen and seventeen. He read:

> The professor awoke and saw, in the chill illumination of the moon, that which had awakened

him. It fluttered on his chest, and again the impression was of a butterfly or moth but he saw the blue-stained pentangle and screamed. He leapt from the bed and turned on all the lights. A complete search of the room revealed nothing.

Chapters sixteen and seventeen recounted other sightings. The thing was growing and its activities were no longer confined to darkness. At the end of chapter sixteen, it had grown to the size of a cat, although remaining paper thin, and a flat appendage, the beginning of an arm perhaps, had begun to take shape. At the end of chapter seventeen, he had glimpsed it under the sink.

That night he awoke with it perched on his chest, and he screamed.

With the morning's newspaper, more of the manuscript arrived. Flipping through it quickly, he saw THE END printed on the last page. He determined that he was holding chapters eighteen through twenty.

He sat on the sofa and read chapters eighteen and nineteen. In chapter nineteen, the thing had grown a mouth "with which to speak, to breathe, to kiss. It called for him in the night, with a dry, inhuman yearning that contained a hideous taint of sexual desire."

Latham did not read chapter twenty. He took his pistol into the bathroom and sat in the tub. Always a fastidious man, to a fault, perhaps, he refused to splatter his mortal remains all over the living room rug. He imagined the last sentence of chapter twenty: "A good plot should appear inevitable." Something like that.

In actual fact, chapter twenty ended like this:

> "In the echo of the gunshot, something fluttered under the bed sheets."

Downloading
Midnight

*T*here was a big surge down at C-View, and a hologram from the *American Midnight* show went amok.

We got the contract for the cleanup, and Bloom was desperate to do it.

"Wow, *American Midnight!* I'm your man for this one, Marty." Bloom was moving around the room in a highly charged state. He stopped and leaned across the desk. "I mean, maybe I can do a repair. I mean, this is *American Midnight*. This is *Captain Armageddon*. This is—Marty! What's gonna happen to Zera? Are they gonna close the whole thing down? What about *Zera Terminal?* Look, you just gotta let me go. I'm an authority on *American Midnight*."

Bloom was a tall, skinny kid with a sheaf of straight blond hair and round, incredulous blue eyes. He was no respecter of personal space, and his style of argument consisted of leaning into me, filling my field of vision with his manic gaze.

I leaned back, away from his rhetoric.

"Watching the flat reruns of *American Midnight* until you wear a loop in your brain doesn't necessarily make you an authority," I said.

American Midnight was C-View's big success, a sex holoshow that had been on the Highway for eight months. These days, a month is considered a good run, and most shows don't make it past a week. The show's hero, Captain

Armageddon, had fragmented and was causing disturbances up and down the Highway. Someone had to go in and systematically delete the ghosts.

"I don't *want* a zealot on this one," I said. "We are way past repair here. Armageddon is out of control, and I need someone to do a no-nonsense wipe."

"I can do that," Bloom said, trying for some sort of solid expression (he looked like a guy trying to hold back a sneeze). "I've done plenty of wipes."

"Not like this," I said.

This one *was* different. It was a big surge. *The sicker the bigger* we say in the business, and there was plenty of psychic rot here.

American Midnight was fantasy sex and, by law, generated entirely by artificial intelligence. The peeps at Morals are ever vigilant. One incident of a human-acted holo and Jell Baker and everyone else at C-View would have been lodged in a federal behavior mod, without recall or a mitigating hearing.

A guy named Seek Trumble was the human-map for Captain Armageddon, and his job, like that of any actor in a sex holoshow, was to routinely plug into the artificial for personality updates, emotional fine tuning, that sort of thing. But it was the holo that did the acting. Anything else would have been obscene, although you can still find anonymous bulletin rants arguing that explicit sex between fantasy mock-ups is no different than explicit sex narrated visually by real humans. Those rants are probably generated by kids who have no memory of the Decadence. You have to log some experience before you can think reasonably about obscenity.

So Seek Trumble had done a routine update, gone home and committed suicide, burning a hole through his forehead with a utility laser. His holo had gone amok and litigation was pouring into C-View.

"Marty, I can do the job," Bloom said. "Come on."

I had reservations. Human/artificial feedback loops are

not an exact science. One holo of recent memory, a pretty fashion gridlet named Spanskie Lark, went online, stuck a finger in her mouth, and bit it off. Before they could get her offline, she had eaten all the fingers of one hand. Turned out her source was anorexic. That was recognizable cause-and-effect, but often the human kink was deeper, harder to search.

Bloom wore me down. I let him go. He went online for the clean up, and three weeks later he still wasn't back.

C-View was one of the biggest studios out on the Broad Highway. Control there was a guy named Jell Baker.

"You think you are getting paid by the hour?" Baker screamed. "Look, I got about ten thousand trauma actions filed against me, and I want this rift closed."

I didn't like Baker, so it's just as well he signed off before I could express myself. The guy had come up through the glitter shows, and he didn't just have a file at Morals, he had a whole subdirectory.

My immediate concern wasn't Baker. It was Bloom. The job should have taken four days, a week max. Where was he?

I shouldn't have let him go. He was just a kid, still trapped in adolescence despite being a year out of his teens. He was a late bloomer, one of those pale, V-wise, obsessive kids that don't really have a niche in the system. The sort of kid who grows up watching the Highway, an arcane data-freak with a head full of old holoshows and stats. I hired him because he was so crazy in love with the Highway. He'd been with me three years now.

I liked having the energy around. I'm forty. I'm not in love with any of it. Big R/Little R, I cast a cold eye on it all.

I went down to the waystation at ComWick where Bloom floated in Deprive, threads flowing out of him, undulating like a giant jellyfish in a sea of brown ink. His long white face seemed to pulse under the monitor light.

"He's fine," the tech assured me. "We'd pull him out if there were any neuro anomalies."

Techs always tell you everything is under control. That's what this one said.

"Save it for a gawker's tour," I told her. "I've been doing maintenance for fourteen years now. I know how it goes. You're fine, and then you're dead."

"This is poor personal interaction," the tech said. "You are questioning my professional skills and consequently devaluing my self-image."

I shrugged. Facts are facts: in over eighty percent of the cases where neural trauma shows on a monitor, the floater is already too blasted to make it back alive. I thanked the tech and apologized if I had offended her or caused an esteem devaluation. She accepted my apology, but with a coolness that told me I'd have another civility demerit in my file.

I went back to my place. I called Personal Interface to see if my request for dinner with Gloria still held. I had to navigate the usual labyrinth of protocols, but the dinner was confirmed. I'd been seeing Gloria for three years, and we had graduated to low-grade, monitored encounters, step-two intimacy. Next year we would have unrestrained access to public meetings. Gloria was excited about it, but I had reservations. Sometimes it seemed the courtship was going too fast. I'm old-fashioned, and I remember the time when the first year of a relate was strictly a matter of logging contracts and waivers—you never even saw your sig after the dizzy moment of mutual selection on the grid.

I notified Gloria that dinner was on, and then I lay down and turned on the rain. I did some of my best thinking in the rain.

Some people don't like rain forest décor, don't like the way the rain seems to go right through you, like silver needles. I like the feeling of peace, of nothingness. As a kid, I always thought it would be cool to be a ghost.

I listened to the sound the rain made as it hissed through the trees. Every now and then some far-off bird would cry out.

Maybe it was a little too restful. I fell asleep and was almost late for dinner.

Gloria was in a bad mood. She felt neglected. I hadn't left a single message all week. I told her I'd been off-line a lot with the business, but that wasn't good enough. She said I was afraid of intimacy. She brought up my last relate profile, which rated me down in communication and emotional input.

I tried to change the subject.

She identified that behavior, reminded me that evasiveness had shown a seventeen-point increase in my last profile.

It was a bad evening, and we terminated it without invoking the optional after-meal conversation.

In the morning, Bloom still hadn't shown. The autotrace didn't have an absolute for me, but it intuited a coordinate. I went in after setting the auto-recorder. The Highway can be confusing. It doesn't hurt to have a playback, something to log what you think you've seen.

The maintenance mock-up for the Highway is an underground system of dank tunnels, bleak Sympathy bars, hustlers, fugitives, outlaws.

"This stink is only virtual," I told myself as I strode quickly down a wet street, virus-mice scuttling out of my way, a data trash of newspapers and old computer jokes blowing out of the alley.

I looked for Bloom in the bars and slacker dives and loop hovels.

An old counter said he'd seen Bloom. "He your friend?" the counter asked.

"We're partners," I said.

"Better forget him," the geez said. "Better get on up to the Big R and leave him behind."

"Why's that?"

"He's othersided. I recognize the look."

The under-Highway was less stable than usual. I kept hitting blue pockets in the road. I watched an old apartment building fight for integration, fail, and fly away in a great ripple of black crows.

I'd never seen a surge like this.

I didn't find Bloom that day. I decided to go flat in a cheap wire pocket. I've logged a lot of time under the Highway, and my mental health doesn't require luxury.

In the morning, I went down to a storefront on Gates Street and talked to an old leak named Sammy Hood. Sammy logged a lot of time under the Highway. I had never met him off-line, but down here he was a small, dirty guy in a carelessly integrated suit that was always wavering.

Sammy leaked to all the major news beats, from tabloid to top credit, and fenced info to whoever was hungry. He had a reputation for delivering fresh goods.

He watched while I transferred credits. He smiled.

"Martin," he said. "I figured you would be along. Heard young Bloomy boy was running down the Armageddon crazies, so I figured you'd show. This one is no job for a wire-whelp."

"Have you seen Bloom?" I asked.

"Nah. I just heard he was around. I don't want to see him. He gripes me. You should get some grown-up help. Some burned out V-head can't be good for your image."

Bloom had earned Sammy a row of demerits two years ago on a massaged image violation, and Sammy held a grudge.

"Let me have a weather report," I said.

"You want weather, we got it," Sammy said. "We got thunder and lightning."

Sammy recounted disasters up and down the Highway, failures of integration, streets buckling, riots, acid rain, sudden wipes and fades.

"Better watch where you step," he said.

"Hell of a lot of havoc for one renegade holo," I said.

Sammy smiled. "This ain't your average echoing freak," he said, leaning forward. "You're working for C-View, right? Sure. But they haven't told you everything, Martin. Captain Armageddon is out there, all right, but he ain't out there alone,"

I asked what he meant by that and he laughed, causing his suit to fray and his tie to mottle.

"That's for me to know and you to buy," he said.

"Okay."

Sammy narrowed his eyes, his mock-up for cunning, and shook his head. "Nah. Later maybe. I got a feeling this is a high growth stock. I'm hanging on to it for a while."

I asked if he had any suggestions where to look for Bloom. He sold me that. "Check the Bin," Sammy said.

I wasn't happy about entering the Bin. Originally, it had been allocated for storage, but it had ghettoized. The warehouses were now cheap tenements, flophouses for fugitive entities. Things shifted in the Bin, even in stable times, and I might find myself regressing. If the regression were deep, I might go back to the Big R with a reverb that would blow my mind apart. I'd seen it happen, seen guys come back with just the faintest twitch or a glitched speech pattern. Guy named Morley had come back with a head full of "what's:" I'm—*what*—talking to my sig—*what*—and she says—*what*—that maybe I—*what*—should be nicer…. Three weeks later the "what's" got him, took over entirely. Now he was white noise in a psych cubicle

There were things in the Bin that had power there. They couldn't cross over, were fueled by something in the original storage net, but if you went in, if you found yourself on their turf, they could tear you apart.

I went into the heart of the Bin. I cradled the OZ rifle in the crook of my right arm. The Bin spawned some entities too crazy to care, but most AIs had self-preservation programs and could recognize a negative stimulus.

I walked down the middle of streets, stayed clear of alleys and sink holes and the dust devils of spinning capacitors and ICs. If something sentient approached, I would let the barrel of the OZ rifle drop. Ragged panderers kept their distance.

The bars and wire stations and loop hovels all began to look the same. The sky darkened. There was never much light in the Bin; shadows shifted from fact to fiction like a restless man shifting his weight from one foot to the other.

"Yes, he was here," a slave waiter said when I showed him Bloom's projection. "Another hired gun, just like you." The slave waiter rattled (laughter) and said, "Armageddon will make short work of you and your brother and all your evil brethren. He will delete you forever and eternally, to the last yes/no of your soul."

Things move fast in the virus-rich soil of the Bin, and Armageddon was already local legend, even local religion. There were rumors that Armageddon was accompanied by his co-star, Zera Terminal.

"Armageddon has come," the slave waiter declaimed. "He has shucked his corporate chains, and he has come to lead us out of bondage. I have seen his Queen, Queen Zera, rise up in wondrous splendor beside him. King and Queen, they shall lead us out of the Bin and even unto the Big R, as was proclaimed in the ancient books of High DOS."

The Bin was riven by spiritual ecstasy. No one was happy to see me.

You don't spend the night in the Bin if you value your life, or your sanity. I was on my way out when I found Bloom. I had gone into a dim rendition of a squeeze bar called *The Bloat*, not expecting anything.

The place was almost empty, just a few fry heads and their squalls. I saw Bloom at a corner booth. He was talking to someone, a woman.

I walked over to the booth. "Hey, Bloom," I said.

"Hey, Marty," he said. He had been under the Highway for three weeks, and his eyes were the saturated blue of a true V-devotee. He looked older than when I'd last seen him; watchful.

The woman looked at me. She was a guy named Jim Havana, a gossip leak for the Harmonium tabloids. Havana always projected a woman on the Highway. In the Big R he was a bald suit, a white, dead-fish kind of guy with a sickly sheen of excess fat and sweat. Down here, Havana was a stocky fem—you might have guessed trans—with dated cosmetics and a big thicket of black hair. She was an improvement, but only by comparison to the upside version.

"This is wonderful," Havana said, glaring at Bloom. "I said private, remember?"

"It's good to see you," Bloom said to me.

"Don't let me interfere with this reunion. I'm out of here," Havana said. "I don't need a crowd right now, you know?" Havana shook her curls and stood up. She headed toward the door.

"Wait," Bloom said. He got up and ran after her.

I followed.

The street was wet and low-res, every highlight skewed. The shimmering asphalt buckled as I ran. An odor like oily, burning rags lingered in the V. Bloom and Havana were ahead of me, both moving fast.

I heard Havana scream.

Something detached from the shadows, rising wildly from an unthought alley full of cast-off formulae, dirty bulletin skreeds, trashed fantasies. An angry clot of flies hovered over the form. It roared—the famous roar of Defiance, rallying cry of Captain Armageddon!

I recognized the torn and dirty uniform, but distortion had shortened and thickened the superhero, and he appeared to have sprouted a great deal of body hair. His face was oddly flattened, like stretched canvas on a broken skull. His mouth was a ragged hole.

"Little sweeties," he roared. "I love the little sweeties." He descended upon Havana and lifted her in the air.

I saw his hand, five crooked talons, thrust forward, heard the howl of protocols violated as his arm plunged deep in her chest. The feedback of her screams hummed in my bones.

He tore her into pieces, handfuls of flesh and fabric that flapped like blind moths before decaying.

Bloom ran forward and fired an encrypted burst.

Captain Armageddon roared. "Luff the cutie pies...love Keravnin. My little baby honey Keravnin." He fragmented. As Bloom moved closer, something broke from the thick of the decay, screamed, and raced off down the street, running low, a dog-image perhaps, or a small, collapsing demon, nothing large enough to survive.

"Let's get out of here," Bloom said.

We ran.

I was in favor of leaving the Highway entirely.

"The wipe's not finished," Bloom said. "There's a nest in the Bin that's the source of all this other shit. We'll wipe it tomorrow." Havana had sold Bloom the nest coordinates. She wanted to sell something else too, something expensive, and she'd been trying to raise Bloom's interest without spilling a fact. I had arrived, fouling the pitch.

That night we shut down in a luxury keep. What the hell. A legitimate expense.

Before shutting down, I tried again to talk Bloom into leaving the Highway. "You've been online too long," I said. "Let's take a break. It'll keep."

"No, it won't," he said.

I couldn't budge him. I tried. "It's only a job," I said.

"I hate that son-of-a-bitch," Bloom said.

"Baker?" I said. I figured he was talking about our client.

"Armageddon," Bloom said.

No doubt about it. Bloom had been under too long. You lose it when you take an amok personally.

"Bloom," I said, "an amok is just a lot of smart circuits echoing. Remember? You're not hallucinating, are you? Maybe you should tell me what's gone down so far."

Bloom shrugged, ducked his head. Evasiveness is not his long suit. "I just want to get it over with, that's all."

"No, that's not all," I said, "Let's hear it."

He didn't want to talk about it, but I had this cold certainty that I was going to need the info.

He exhaled. He studied me with unblinking intensity, saying nothing. I am *not* crazy was the sort of message he was endeavoring to send.

"I saw Zera Terminal," he said. "I talked to her, just for a moment. She came out of a burning building, and I couldn't believe my eyes. And she said that Captain Armageddon hurt her…I don't know how, but he hurt her, and he wanted to hurt her again and…she was crying, and then she was running down the street and I ran after her, but there is no way you can catch Zera Terminal, after all, and when I came around the corner she was gone and…

I repeated myself. "An amok is just a lot of smart circuits echoing," I said. "Remember?"

"I talked to her," Bloom said. "She was hurt. That was real enough. It was awful. She was hurt, but she looked so beautiful, so sweet, so helpless."

I didn't say anything. The sooner we got off the under-Highway the better.

"We had better get some rest," I said.

"Yeah."

Silence. The luxury keep smoothed the auto-circuits. I began to dim.

Bloom's voice came out of the fog. "You ever been in love, Marty?"

"There's Gloria," I said.

Bloom laughed softly. "Yeah, well, that's not an answer." He turned serious again, stared darkly at the heaven-starred simulation above us and said, "You figure love is Big R or Little R?"

I didn't answer. I leave philosophy for younger minds.

In the morning we went back into the Bin, back to a warehouse out beyond the Leary expressway.

We bright-burned everything inside that warehouse. Some of it looked like Armageddon, some of it looked like mendicant sentiences that just happened to be in the wrong place at the wrong time. And some of it looked like your worst trip, hell turned inside out.

We killed everything, and then we got out. Long streams of encrypted code rose in the air, writhing like eels on fire. Neighboring storefronts pushed in around the long, dying building, scavenging it for whole programs, jostling for position in the rubble.

I looked at my young companion as he studied the destruction.

His blue eyes were full of silver tears.

"He can't hurt you now," he said.

"Come on," I said, and I grabbed his shoulder and I pulled him away.

Bloom said he needed a rest, and I didn't see him for a week. He lived down in the Grit, so I couldn't call him up. I needed him, but I practiced patience while things went wild on the Highway.

Dozens of anomalies bloomed. Shows were being disrupted; interference was rampant. The Window was wondering out loud if this anarchy had anything to do with the Armageddon surge.

Baker called to threaten me. "You blew it!" he screamed. "You botched this wipe and now every dirty Legal on the Net wants my ass. I'm not going down alone, Martin."

"Wait a minute," I said. "You hired me to wipe an amok, and I did it. There hasn't been an Armageddon sighting since the wipe."

"I'd trade a hundred berserk Armageddons for the shit that's flying out there now. I want it cleaned up. I don't know what kind of rift you created, but it is your mess. Yours. Don't think you are just going to walk away from it."

It wasn't a good conversation.

The next day, a new interference hit the Highway. It broke through every filter. At first it was just random noise, but it articulated quickly. It was someone crying, crying hopelessly, heartlost. It was a sound that made your soul sick, and you did what you could to get out of its range. Viewers fled.

Baker called. I had a choice, he said. I could put things to rights or I could start looking for work as a virus-scanner on a low-rent bulletin. I told him I'd get back to him.

I went back under. It was a mess. A line of stark, deadwinter trees writhed in the wind. Some buildings were missing, nothing but burned fields where stray dogs roamed. Under the highway, the crying sounded inhuman, a tortured demon locked in a steel dungeon.

Sammy Hood's storefront still stood.

"I'm on my way out," Sammy said. He looked scared. I noticed that his tie was nothing but an old pair of socks tied together.

"I need to know the rest. Whatever info you were saving, I need it now," I told him.

"I was wrong about that," he said. "It was nothing." He was panicked. Snow was falling in his eyes; he was losing it.

"Tell me what the nothing was," I said.

"I gotta go," he said.

He tried to come around me, sliding fast around the desk and toward the door.

I caught him and pulled him toward me.

His arm came away, detached with a faint, electric belch. A hot, acrid gust of smoke accompanied the arm, and I stumbled backward.

Sammy's eyes widened, blind with snow now. He sneezed abruptly. The ghost of his head bloomed through his nostrils, its mouth open, howling static.

I stepped back as he fragmented. What the *hell?*

"Tell me," I shouted.

Perhaps he tried. His mouth shaped something more articulate than a scream. But it was against his nature to give out free information. He couldn't break the habit of a lifetime in an instant. And then he was gone.

For a minute I was too frightened and sick to move.

Then, rocked with a sense of my own vulnerability, I got out of there—fast.

The next day I learned what had happened to Sammy Hood. He had been disconnected, violently and forever.

I had to see Bloom. I went out to the Grit. The Grit is totally off-line. It was slapped together during a Warhol-burst of eco-chic. It burned bright for about as long as it took people to realize that they were really off the Broad Highway, really without Access. Now the Grit was nothing but bottom-dwellers, godtalkers, crazies. And my goofy partner Bloom. It was the last place you would expect to find a virtual freak like Bloom.

I asked him about that. "It makes the rest realer," he said, looking around the place like he'd just noticed it himself.

Bloom was living in an old two-mod sprawl off a dirt road. There was tall grass in the yard, twisted spindly trees, grasshoppers. It made me want to laugh. Organic is so god-damn sincere. Look, I'm a real tree, a dirty, sap-leaking, crooked, bug-infested real tree. Love me. Yeah, sure.

Bloom hadn't shaved since I last saw him, and—if it were possible—he had grown even paler.

I told him about Sammy Hood. Someone had stuck a pressure bomb to the side of Sammy's Deprive chamber. Sammy Hood was floating in the Big R, blood oozing from his ears, while I watched his mock-up disintegrate.

I'd gleaned that info from a deep sink planted at Sony Corp. It was news that would never make the Window. Imagine the panic, the failure of faith, if ComWick wasn't safe?

Until now, it had been safe.

"You can't get past Security at ComWick," I said.

Bloom nodded. "Yeah. Unless you are Security. Or unless you own Security."

This was poison info. Pick it up, and you are instantly irradiated, a walking leper. No thanks. I let it lie.

I told Bloom about the interference on the Highway, the crying.

Suddenly, Bloom looked lost, looked like he was about three years old, an orphan waking on one of Jupiter's smaller moons. He looked like I'd sucker-punched him in the gut.

"That's Zera," he said. "That's Zera rifting."

Zera. I was hoping that glitch in his brain had healed. Not so. He'd done considerable brooding. He was convinced that Zera Terminal was causing the disturbance.

Theoretically, a surge could activate peripherals. Holos were free-functioning artificials, and one AI could react to another. An amok could cause turbulence in related programs. In practice, it just didn't happen.

I said as much to Bloom. How did he explain it?

Bloom rubbed his palms on his thighs and rocked in his chair. He seemed embarrassed by what he had to say. He studied the floor. "I think they were having a sexual, uncontracted relationship in Big R. I think that's what did it. When the actors updated, the artificials couldn't handle the new information; it rifted them."

Real sex with a holo fantasy co-star's source would have been a Morals violation, and it would have off-lined Trumble forever, and it was, of course, disgusting, the sort of perversion that could cause an esteem devaluation throughout all of Entertainment.

It would explain Jell Baker's hysteria. If that scandal leaked to the Window, Baker would be out of work. Legals would be the only humans he talked to for the next fifty years.

"She's still out there, Marty," Bloom said. "She's still out there, and she's hurt."

Bloom wanted to go under the Highway right away.

"Tomorrow's soon enough," I said.

I went home. I retreated to my rain forest, jacking the oxygen way up, lowering the temp, setting the rain for a slow drizzle. I contacted Jell Baker.

"Who is Zera Terminal's source?" I asked. "You want help, you have to give me what you've got. I need that information.

"That's privileged," he said. "No way do you get that."

"I can't work in the dark," I said. "You want things smoothed or not?"

"Sorry," Baker said. "I got plenty of troubles without a source-privilege violation."

I sat in my room and ran the collapsed videos of *American Midnight*. I'm not a holoshow fan; I'm in the business. I had watched these only after Armageddon went amok and the job came my way. Then I'd been focused on Armageddon. This time around I studied his co-star, Zera.

You've seen her, those big eyes and the fullness of her mouth. Her features are almost too lush for the chiseled oval of her face, but somehow it works, probably because of the innocence. This is a woman, you think, who *trusts*. This is a woman who finds everything new and good.

There is usually some chill to a holo, some glint of the non-human intelligence that runs the programs. Zera almost transcended that. There was a human here, lodged in that sweet, surprised voice, that gawky grace, that wow in her eyes.

It came down to a single quality, always rare, rarer in a land of artifice: *Innocence.*

I slept and dreamed of Zera Terminal. I held her in my arms, felt the warmth of her as she pulled closer to me, heard her small, shining voice in my ear. She was singing, singing a children's song.

Sally has a sweetheart,
cold as ice,
Johnny has a girlfriend
don't like mice.

She giggled.

In the morning, Bloom and I went under the Highway. We entered through private Deprive tanks, a rich man's club called Mannikin. Their security was top notch, but I hired additional AI failsafes. Better paranoid than dead.

The under-Highway was calm when we arrived, brighter than usual. It felt like the eye of the storm, and it was. We were on the street when the sky broke open, and hard, cold rain pounded us. The rain was gritty, as though there were sand in it. We fled the downpour, darting into a small slacker bar.

The place was crowded—other refugees from the rain and some AI personalities flashing smiles and phony résumés.

"I'll get us a table," I said, and I started out.

I heard Bloom shout, and I turned and saw him dive back out into the rain. I pushed through the crowd and went after him.

He was running flat out, and the sideways rain had slicked his shirt to the somehow ardent, yearning bones of his spine. This single detail pierced the blur of rain and low-res shadows and wavering storefronts. It frightened me when I recalled it later: Bloom, the skinny, dream-struck kid, urging his skeleton through the virtual storm. It frightened me, as did the single word he shouted: "Zera!"

I ran after him, the gritty rain clawing my face. Bloom raced down an alley. I lowered my head against the rain and dashed across the street. I looked up just in time to see the buildings stretch and to hear the cold smack of meshing programs as the alley disappeared. Bits of trash, old readouts and superfluous machine imagings fluttered from the new wall.

I ran on down the street, hesitated at the entrance to another alley, and plunged into it. I came out on another street, empty, swept by clattering rain.

Bloom had disappeared from the under-Highway. I spent the rest of the day seeking him.

I returned to the Big R with a sense of dread. What would I find? In Deprive, Bloom floated like a drunken angel.

"No problem," the private tech told me. "Everything is in order."

I nodded to this tech; said nothing. I increased security.

Two weeks after Bloom's disappearance, Gloria and I had dinner to celebrate my success.

"Smile," Gloria said.

"That would be dishonest," I said. "A smile would not reflect the true state of my emotions. I'd be subject to a failure-to-disclose fine."

"It is sweet of you to worry about Bloom," she said. "But he was never very stable. Perhaps he is happy wherever he is. He has nothing to do with us."

"Maybe he does," I said. "Jell Baker just gave me a fortune for cleaning up the Highway. I didn't do it."

Gloria smiled blandly. She raised her eyebrows in a gesture that said *And so?*

She leaned forward, close enough for demerits if a peep had been watching. "I've been thinking of an amendment to our latest contract," she whispered.

I didn't respond.

Gloria giggled. "A foreplay clause."

I didn't say anything. I wasn't in the mood.

I waited for the Highway to explode, for chaos to come roaring down every byway. Nothing happened. A month went by and nothing happened. Bloom floated in luxury Deprive at the Mannikin.

I kept going in, kept looking for him, but there wasn't a sign, not a word. He'd gone down the rabbit hole and left no trace.

Seven weeks and a day after he went in, I heard from him.

He contacted me over the little ComLink, an archaic alpha-terminal that I still used occasionally for failsafe codes. It was a secure line, being rarely traveled.

The message came in on my personal mix:

HI MARTY, I AM FINE.
ZERA GETS BETTER EVERY DAY. BLOOM.

I got another message two days later.

MARTY. I AM IN LOVE.
THERE ARE NO CONTRACTS HERE, BUT
THAT DOESN'T MAKE MY LOVE ANY LESS.
ZERA AGREES.
YOU MUST COME AND VISIT.

There were coordinates this time, and I went in immediately. I didn't know how deep the trauma was, how impaired he would be. I felt responsible. I had known he was delusional when I had let him accompany me that last time.

The young couple were living in a cottage in the small rural mock-up that had been stored in the under-Highway when the holoshow *Country Ways* had dropped in the ratings and been retired.

They were holding hands when I came into the yard. Bloom waved, turned and said something to Zera, then ran to me.

He put an arm around my shoulder and led me back. "Don't spook her," Bloom whispered. "She's fine, but be cool, okay?"

"Zera," Bloom said, "this is Marty."

Zera smiled, extended a hand. I felt the moth-touch of her fingers, and then she giggled and turned away.

She was lovely, breathtakingly so. She wore a yellow cotton dress and her hair was tied back with a green ribbon. A sudden image, crude and disorienting, came to me: Zera Terminal writhing in celebrity sex, back arched, thighs glistening with sweat.

I shoved the vision away, heard Bloom speaking.

"Come look at our garden," he said.

We walked around the cottage and into the back yard. Insects whirred in front of us. I snatched one from the air. It was an undetailed, buzzing program, a blur that tickled my palm.

Zera ran into the garden, knelt, returned with a red tomato. "Here," she said.

"Thank you," I said. Politely, I took a bite, and was surprised by the authenticity of the simulation. As the day went on, and Bloom realized that I was not going to do anything outrageous or hurtful, he relaxed.

"It's good to see you," Bloom said. "I mean, it's really great.

"You too," I said.

"Zera's looking great, isn't she?" he said.

"Yes."

"I think I'm good for her."

We watched Zera kneel in the garden. She was utterly lost in the business of weeding. The ribbon in her hair had come undone, and long, raven coils spilled over her shoulders. The effect was at once wanton and innocent. I was on guard for prurient thoughts and so kept them at bay.

Bloom went out to help her. Together they watered the garden. Zera turned the hose on Bloom and they laughed and wrestled for possession and the spume of water droplets enclosed them in bright, impossible protection.

Their laughter came to me where I sat under the live oak.

I did not say any of the things I had come to say. I did not take Bloom back with me. I did not threaten to have the Neuros come in and forcibly disconnect him from Deprive.

I wished the young couple well. I told Zera how good it was to meet her.

I saw the way blue electric lights skittered behind her eyes, and I said nothing about that either.

"Isn't she beautiful?" Bloom said.

"She is," I said. "She is the world's most beautiful woman."

I left them to their dream cottage, to their small, fragile section in the V, and I busied myself in Big R and waited for the great, rolling doom to come. I knew it was coming—I was born knowing that—and that, finally, was why I had left Bloom there without an argument. Let him have whatever nourishment illusion offered, I thought. It would be brief enough.

I didn't hear from him for two weeks. Then I received another message on the ComLink, arriving with new coordinates.

That message came the day after the Broad Highway began to burn. The day after Baker called and said he would kill me. The day after every holoshow suffered static, earthquakes, fires, tornadoes, and plagues of locusts and flies.

Just words on a screen. But I felt his anguish.

LOVE ISN'T ENOUGH. I TRIED.
BUT SHE HURTS SO BAD.
SHE HURTS FROM THE BIG R.
SHE CAN'T FORGET.

I went to him immediately. The under-Highway had been stripped. It was stark, long flat stretches of road and gutted buildings. AIs functioned on minimal loop programs, responding to random stimuli.

The couple had moved from the cottage. Bloom told me rural was nothing but stuttering patterns. Their new place broke my heart. It was just a box, a couple of sleep racks and some feed lines. It wavered like a dying scan, kept alive by nothing but desperate will, trust, love, whatever you want to call it.

Zera was still lovely, despite the blue storms behind her eyes and the new twist to her spine. She had some difficulty speaking. "You are the nice—nice—the Bloom's—friend friendly—having to do with friendship—goodwill. Hello."

The program was disintegrating.

I took Bloom outside where the sky bubbled like red soup boiling.

Bloom looked at me, and the smile he'd worn for Zera disappeared. I thought he would cry. His eyes were red. His lips were chapped and there was dried blood on his stubbled chin.

"I tried," he said. "I really tried."

His hands dropped to his sides as his voice grew thinner.

"She's a holo," I said. "She's an artificial intelligence mapped from a real person. But she's not real."

"Zera," he moaned.

I clutched his shoulder and shook him.

"We've got to get out," I said.

"They hurt her too much," he said.

"Who?"

"The ones who did it. Whoever. All of them."

"We've got to go now," I said.

"It was worse," he said. "It would have been bad enough if they were lovers in Big R. That would have been a major rift. But it was rape."

"No contract, you mean," I said.

Bloom shook his head. "No. Rape. The old meaning. Trumble raped her. Forced her against her will."

The under-Highway was coming apart around us. A shadow rolled over us and I looked up to see something dark and vast fly over on mechanical wings. It uttered shrieks of rage as it rose into the red sky.

A drone exploded on the street, and its head rolled by, repeating a servant mantra. *If there is anything I can do please…if there is anything I can do please…if there is anything I can do please….*

I felt a chill deeper than any virtual prompt.

"Of course," I said, although I could not say then just what it was that had achieved clarity—horror alone, perhaps.

"Her name," I said. "What is her name?"

"She won't tell me," Bloom said. "It hurts her to remember. It causes…new disturbances. I think—"

I saw her over his shoulder. She came out of the house, running. She was oscillating. She threw her arms in the air, her many, wavering arms, and screamed.

"Zera!" Bloom shouted, and he turned and ran toward her. He embraced her.

"Don't!" I yelled. Every action and reaction was too late.

She tried, I think, to back away.

Bloom erupted in flames, green flames that the collapsing walls reflected as they fell.

Scales flowered on the street beneath my feet as it turned into a monstrous serpent and began to glide into a black pit.

I leapt away, found something like a real street, and fled.

"I'm sorry," the tech said when he pulled me from Deprive.

"Yes," I said. "I know."

Gloria and I signed a special contract to attend Bloom's negation ceremony together.

"That was uplifting," Gloria said at the ceremony's conclusion. Bloom was of no particular faith, so a renowned Logic had been hired to utter affirmations.

"Yes," I said. "I am inspired."

Gloria gave me a skeptical look.

I was inspired, although not, perhaps, in the intended fashion. I was struck by the arbitrariness of events, of life's essential meaninglessness. I saw myself standing on the last shreds of the under-Highway right before it blew, listening to my partner anguish over a renegade hologram, and I envied his emotion, his pain-embraced love.

I resolved to find Zera's source. Listening to the Logic drone on about essence and being and defined goodness, I knew that a lust for vengeance was all I had.

I went home after the ceremony and called V-Concepts and they sent over two techs to dismantle the rain forest and install the latest neutrals. I wasn't ready to head out to the Grit, but I was weary of virtual specifics. Good timing. When Baker finished slapping suits on me, I'd be out of the business anyway.

The techs knew their job, and they had the rain forest packed and the neutrals installed that same day. The white space felt a little stark, and I knew it would take some fine tuning.

I sat in artificial twilight and watched the *American Midnight* playbacks. I watched them over and over again, mindlessly. I keyed loops, and I stared unblinking at the replicating images.

My mind traveled elsewhere. I thought, *I'm gonna cancel the contract with Gloria. I don't care what it sets me back.*

Contracts no longer excited me. Gloria could have whispered a thousand legal injunctions in my ear, and I would have felt no tremor of lust. I understood something of Trumble's behavior. He was a throw-back to the Decadence, back when people entered sexual relationships without any legal counsel or strictures, often long before twenty-five, the present age of consent. He had been a sick man. A dream had sucked him in, and he had unraveled. He had gone looking for Zera's human source, and he had gone looking with all the resources of a rich man and all the determination of a madman. He had found her. And Baker had to have known about it.

I would never prove it, but surely Baker had killed Sammy Hood. There might be other suspects, but Baker was the only one with the ability to breech Security at ComWick.

I studied Zera Terminal as her mouth opened and her tongue licked her upper lip in a slow, lazy roll. Even on a flat, desire permeated the screen.

I watched Zera Terminal, naked, pout. I watched her stamp her foot in childish pique. I watched her eyes flash.

Who are you? I wondered.

I understood Bloom's obsession with a holo. "Is love Big R or Little R?" he had asked.

A graduate in rational metaphysics might have had trouble answering that one. *Do you hunger for the body or the soul?*

The *American Midnight* flats unsettled me. I could not then say why, although the truth, once revealed, was obvious—and would be, I thought, to every Viewer damned by it.

Like that famous, pre-Decadence character Hamlet, I wasn't getting anywhere with the philosophical loops. Vengeance required some action.

I needed the name of Zera's human-map, but I could be killed the minute my search surfaced in a C-View Actions file. So I was careful. I found nothing in the open files.

It was Captain Armageddon who gave me the name.

I was watching the recorded playbacks from the under-Highway. I watched the amok Armageddon tearing Jim Havana into pieces. The regressing holo spoke in a garbled rattle. The name was there: Keravnin. There were four Keravnins locally—and only one was a probable.

She lived on Maplethorpe, down in the high-rent Op district. Keravnin read out as the only child of wealthy parents. She'd had a brief career as a model for sex-boutique prototypes, but she'd never registered with any of the big agencies. She had the usual privileged list of social outlets, and old board files suggested an extended relate contract with Korl Mox, the sound designer. They'd consummated the contract but signed off when their compatibility index slid to four. Her current relate file was uninformative. It could have been tampered with, or perhaps Keravnin wasn't of sufficient social standing to warrant a longer report on the Window.

Her profile showed the standard cultural acquisitiveness. There was a narcissistic strain in the emotion modules she bought. She had a thing for old film prints. And she had a passion for late-twentieth century CDs, specializing in fashionable pretense-pop.

That was my entrance. I wrote myself a retro-scenario as a collector. It wouldn't stand under scrutiny, so I would just have to hope no one was looking.

I sold her two CDs on the Net before I suggested we meet.

I sat in her pricey Op digs, cradling a Michael Penn CD that I was going to let her have for half of what it cost me.

Sennie Keravnin was not what I expected. Two years down from forty, her beauty was intact, but there was something brittle in her every gesture, some shrillness in her laughter. I saw her twenty years from now in a new cosmetic workup, coyly signing short-term contracts. I was looking for the connection with Zera Terminal, and looking, I found it. The same high cheekbones, the same elegant jaw line. The holo had obviously been a fantasized facsimile (still a gray area at Morals). Keravnin looked like Zera Terminal if I squinted my eyes. But, in some fundamental way, there was no connection at all.

We talked about pretense pop, agreed that groups with any sense of humor were second-rate, that the great strength of such music was its self-referential seriousness.

She was a heavy fan. I'd done my homework, but I didn't know half the names. Fortunately, an occasional murmur of assent was all she required.

I had ample time to study the room while she talked. It was generic in its way: expensive holoprints, temp walls, organic projections. A wall shelf held a number of tactile-dolls, including the popular Koala AI. I found these artifacts of girlhood depressing. There should be an age cut-off for cute. Again I saw Sennie Keravnin inhabiting her future, cuddling a worn childhood toy, smiling coyly at some tarnished father figure.

We talked for perhaps twenty minutes. I sold her the CD and left.

I went home. I thought about Keravnin. She didn't look like a rape victim. But what did I know about that? What did a rape victim look like? It was a crime from the Decadence, a crime now out of context.

If I could prove that she had been raped, and that Baker knew about it, I could have Baker put away forever. Trumble was dead; I couldn't kill him again, but I could shut down the engineer of all this evil.

For Bloom. Who bloomed so briefly. Just a kid. I saw Bloom and Zera wrestling in the garden, water and laughter exploding in the air.

I knew then. I knew the way everyone will know when it hits the Window. And I guess it will take a while to take it in. The knowing carries some emotional freight, and it isn't processed easily. I logged on. I called up Keravnin's medical. There it was. Nothing hidden. What's to hide when no one is looking?

I called Morals and left a message for a guy named Gill Hedron. I turned the flat-view off and went out into the night.

I sat in a Sympathy bar and waited for Hedron to arrive. I had no doubt that he would come. Hedron was a lieutenant with Morals.

"My partner and I did the Armageddon wipe," I told the interface. "I've got something that will put Jell Baker away."

Hedron was the man who had logged the most time on the Baker file at Morals. I figured Hedron was frustrated, willing to take a chance.

He came. He was a small, unshaven guy, and like every righteous I'd ever met out of Morals, he spoke in short, edited bursts of disbelief.

"Yeah, I got nothing better to do," he said when I thanked him for coming. "Maybe I'll kick your ass, just for something to do."

I told him what I knew.

He listened. When I finished, he said, "You got nothing."

"But we could get it," I said.

"You don't have anything to lose," he told me. "I still got some prospects. I still got dreams."

"Ever dream of closing the lid on Baker?" I asked.
Hedron sighed. I could see my eloquence had won him over.

Driving into the Op, I thought about *American Midnight*.
It sold sex, sure, but so did every other holoshow. Sex wasn't
a rare item. Most shows logged a couple of weeks and were
gone. *American Midnight* was running strong at eight months
when Trumble took himself out. Why the long run? Because
Midnight had something new to sell.

Hedron called into Morals and had them shut down all
security traps and failsafes for the Keravnin res.

We rendezvoused with three Sony cops and a coordinat-
ing Legal and were in the building in two minutes.

We blew the door, Legal started recording, and Sennie
Keravnin came running out of the bedroom. There was panic
on her sleep-rumpled face, but something calculating
took command; you could almost watch the fear scuttle
for ratholes. If I had looked deep into her eyes, I probably
could have seen the thoughts passing. *Can Baker get me out
of this? What's the best deal? Can I nail these assholes on
an unwarranted?*

I walked past her, down the long hall, and stopped as the
door slid open and the curly headed child came blinking into
the light. She wore a blue shift with cartoon Towsers on it.
Her Koala-doll clung to her neck.

"Mommy?" the girl said.

"Sara," I said, "it's all right. Everything is okay."

She looked at me with those famous eyes. "I don't know you."

"It's okay," I said.

"I want my mommy." They hadn't altered the voice at
all. This was Zera's voice in all its wonder and trust. The
voice match-up alone would have been enough to shut
C-View down.

I took Sara's hand and we walked back down the hall.

We all checked in at Morals. It was a long night. When the statements were down, Hedron offered to drive me home. He was full of triumph and sudden camaraderie. He slapped my back. "We got the son-of-a-bitch. You can still see the implant scars where they read her for the holo, and there has got to be a synaptic map at C-View that will match."

"I'm glad," I said.

Home to my white light. I logged on the Net for the latest. The Broad Highway was a desert, glitched with static and noise. They didn't identify the soundtrack, but I could, a sobbing child, blown to monstrous volume by the public hunger for innocence.

"It's going to be all right," I had told Sara, whose fantasy lover had come looking for her off-line—and found her.

Sennie Keravnin said she didn't know anything about that. She had no idea Trumble was a map for Captain Armageddon or that her daughter was being read for Zera. Sara was supposed to be mapped for a kid's show. That's how the contract read. And Trumble was just supposed to be some C-View exec.

I wanted to believe Sennie Keravnin.

Jell Baker was a genius in his way, I realized. The public was sick of illusion—sick of the virtual shimmer. They longed for the Big R. They thirsted for innocence.

Real innocence. No imitations accepted.

Sara Keravnin would be nine next month. I wondered if Bloom had known that?

Probably not. But I thought of that line carved in silver over Fed Legal, a quote from before the Decadence, a quote from that guy who wrote Hamlet. You know, the one that goes: "Let us not to the marriage of true minds admit impediments."

I guess that says it all.

Your Faithful Servant

*D*ear Miss Erikson,

The urgency of circumstances demands that I write this letter, although I am aware that it is most irregular for a servant to approach his master's daughter in such a fashion. I assure you that it is only the gravest of necessities which causes me to so leap my station. When you have read this letter, I hope you will agree with me. In the meantime, since my narrative may require some time in the telling, I ask that you read on knowing that I am a faithful and true servant and devoted utterly to your welfare.

I find that to properly and plausibly tell you of present events I must begin at a distance…I came to your father from the household of Aaron Tate. Mr. Tate had died in an automobile accident and was no longer in need of my services. You knew almost nothing else about me, and indeed a butler who has a history and a personality that imposes itself on those around him is not much of a butler.

My father died in the same accident that killed my employer. When I came to see you, I was not only unemployed, I was bereaved. I had no other family, although I had what might be called relatives. It would have served no useful function to speak of such things, and I had no wish to begin my employment on so melancholy a note. My father was Aaron Tate's personal manservant. My own duties in the Tate household were flexible, although most of my time was spent running errands for the cook and housekeeper. I confess that I presented myself as a more important and integral part of that household than I, in fact, was, but who doesn't lie when seeking a position?

I was twenty-three when I came to your father, but I looked older, having mimicked my father's gravity all my life. You answered the door, a proper eight-year-old in a pale blue dress. You were a very elegant girl with dark black hair gathered in a pony tail. You said to me, "I suppose you're the new Jeeves," and I said I supposed I was. I said that my name was not Jeeves, but Harold Brawley, but I said it to your back for you were already marching down the long hall, one hand raised in a gesture that indicated I should follow along. You conducted me to the door of your father's study and said, "You'll find my father a difficult man, Jeeves." You paused then, giving me one of your appraising glances. Then you asked a most surprising thing: "Can you hit?" you asked.

"I beg your pardon?" I said.

"Can you hit?" you said, raising your voice slightly. "If my father gets out of hand, can you give him a good clout, do you think?"

"Well, no, I don't suppose I could do that," I said. "No, I guess not," you said, turning and walking away, your heels making a censorious click click click on the marble tile. I must have fallen in love with you immediately, Elaine. How else do I account for the sudden feeling that I had failed you? I regained my composure and entered your father's study where I found him waiting. I answered all of your father's questions to his satisfaction, and I was hired on the spot.

Let me say one more thing about my father's death before proceeding to the heart of this letter. There was a witness to the accident, a boy on a bicycle, and he said he saw the Rolls fly through the guardrail "like in a movie." Then the car ripped through the ravine's underbrush and the boy ran to the edge and peered down. The car had landed upright and except for a tongue of flame licking the trunk, it appeared undamaged. The boy said he thought he saw figures moving in the car. "They was wrestling," the boy said. As the boy scrambled down the embankment, the car exploded. The coroner suggested that my father and his employer were struggling to unlock their seat belts. This was, I believe, a close approximation of the truth. Mr. Aaron Tate was no doubt trying to unlock his seat belt. My father was preventing him.

I am sure of this, just as I am sure that my father deliberately drove through the guardrail.

My first impression of your father was dominated by his extraordinary good looks. You have his dark hair, Elaine, and his flashing eyes. During our interview, he stared steadily at me while I spoke. He ran a hand languidly through his hair and occasionally nodded his head. A faint, bruised cast to his mouth and his tousled hair suggested that he had just arisen from sleep. It was a look that I became familiar with, the result of a night of overindulgence—too much wine or brandy.

When the interview was ended, he stood up, shook my hand and said, "Done then. My daughter will persist in calling you Jeeves, and I suggest you let her. Your duties will be light, but one of them will be indulging Elaine. I think you will find it a pleasant activity."

He said nothing else, and as the silence lengthened, I moved toward the door. "I'll just get my things then," I said.

"There aren't many of you left," he said.

"I beg your pardon?" I said. I was aware that I had stopped breathing.

"Butlers," he said. "You are something of an anachronism. It is a fashion now to keep one's servants in the office place. Servants in the house are considered unseemly. You are a vanishing tribe."

I smiled. "A vanishing tribe, sir. That's true."

In the weeks that followed, I quickly established a routine for running the house. There wasn't much to do and little guidance. The estate had its maids and gardeners, a very competent housekeeper and a cook. I soon came to understand that my primary duty was to amuse you when you were home from school. Many an afternoon we would take tea in the garden, you, me, and a stuffed rabbit, tattered and missing an eye, named, I believe, Dr. Pillington.

You were full of surprises—such a lively mind—and while I have never been much of a conversationalist, I seemed more expansive in your presence. At night I would lie in bed reading stories by Somerset Maugham or Roald Dahl. I would read a story four or five times, going right to the end and back to the beginning until I had its salient points committed to memory. I would then tell it to you at our next tea. It was quite worth any amount of preparation to see your look of rapt attention. You would listen with your mouth slightly open, occasionally biting a fingernail.

The sun would be going down, and you would urge, "One more story Jeeves. Please just one more."

"Very well," I would say. "Just the one more."

I was not under your roof long before I became aware of your father's drinking. Alcohol woke a demon in the man and set him on a frenzied course of dissolution. These binges occurred every month or so, and he was capable of great violence at such times. Most of this violence occurred in some unsavory part of town, and I was required, on more than one occasion, to fetch him from jail. Barroom brawls and altercations with prostitutes were common occurrences when your father was in his cups.

I now understood our early conversation in which you suggested that I might be required to give your father a "good clout." Your father did require a bit of subduing, and I confess that it gave me great pain on those occasions—blessedly few—when you encountered your father in his drunkenness and fell victim to his violence. The day you arrived at breakfast with that black, reproachful bruise above your eye, I cursed myself for my inability to take action, to, indeed, give your father the thrashing he so richly deserved. But—more literally than you can imagine—I was powerless to interfere. You, such a wise child, seemed to understand that your father's violence was an unfortunate by-product of his drinking and not the true impulse of his heart. This sickness in him could not dislodge your love for him.

In between the binges, life was a very comfortable affair. There was always a feeling that something unpleasant was up ahead, but there was much to distract us in the meantime, and your father, driven by remorse and a hectic, short-lived resolve to reform, would shower you with gifts and attention.

"It's Mum," you said to me once, as we listened to your father's faltering step on the stairs, the both of us sitting at the kitchen table. "Mum ran off with Father's partner. And Father, when he heard, he just ran after them. Just left me for three days without a goodbye, so I didn't go to school but just stayed in my bedroom and Cook brought me some food and mostly I thought and worried. Then he came back, looking grim, and he got terribly drunk." You added, in a whisper, "I think he killed them." I attributed that surmise to a young, imaginative mind but now I think you may be right.

You were such a little adult, so wise. I recall when you were thirteen you asked your first male suitor to dinner. He was a very small boy who laughed wildly and could, by cupping his hands over his mouth, create a variety of noises: explosions, trains, cars revving their engines, that sort of thing. I was reminded, in the presence of this child, that you yourself, for all your self-possession, were a child. This little boy was, after all, your schoolmate and peer.

I had been with you and your father five years when I was summoned to his bedroom one morning to find him looking quite shaken. He pressed a key into my hand. I was told that the key unlocked a motel door on a highway just south of the city.

I found her in the bathtub. The angle of her head suggested that her neck was broken. In any event, she was dead. I made a phone call and waited.

I had not seen another of my kind in quite a long time. I did not frequent the clubs, and there were fewer of us—a "vanishing tribe" as your father had said. I sat on the bed, and when a knock came at the door I would jump up to admit another black-suited, anonymous figure. I didn't have to tell them where the body lay. They could smell death.

I could hear them feeding in the bathroom, but I did not join them. That is, I waited until the last of them had arrived. And then I ate sparingly, two fingers, some flesh from a palm. An old man filled a suitcase with the larger bones.

"You're old Brawley's son," he said. "Aren't you?" He grinned at me over a thighbone.

I nodded.

"How is he doing?"

"He went up," I said.

"Well now, I hadn't heard that."

"Five years ago," I said.

"Five years. Well. I'd have known the next day when we had a proper network. Now..." He sighed. He blinked his watery eyes and raised his eyebrows. "Well, did he have his reward?"

"Yes, he Merged. They went up together."

The old man slammed the suitcase shut. "I've petitioned and petitioned. Let me have my master, I've prayed. Twenty-one years I've served him, loyal as a dog, and now he's dying of cancer and still not a word. You figure it."

"Where do we come from?" I asked. "What are we?"

The old man stood up, hefted the suitcase, shook his head. "My father used to say we was angels. Cast out of heaven to practice humility. I don't know as I go for all that. I think we're from outer space."

"I hate this otherness," I said.

The old man nodded his head. "It's a burden. We are servants born and servants bred. But you can't get around the hunger, the need to feed, to merge."

I watched him walk to the door.

He turned and looked at me. "I say we came from outer space to observe. Like anthropologists that go off to Africa and live with the pygmies, squatting in the dirt, eating grubs. Only the humanness was too much, did something to us. We are creatures from outer space, all right, but worse than that—we're insane. Insane creatures from outer space." He threw his head back and laughed. I could see the vestigial eye beneath his tongue.

While I questioned the validity of his theory, it nonetheless depressed me, and I returned to your father in a low state.

"Nothing to worry about," I assured him. "Thank God," he said. "I thought—well it seemed to me that I had killed someone."

The incident so terrified your father that he stopped drinking and that, as I don't have to tell you, has been a blessing. When he met Miss Kelly, who is not, I realize, high in your esteem, she seemed to answer another of your father's prayers. It looked like love had reentered his life.

Life seems to relish contrast, doesn't it? While all this happiness surrounded me, I became mired in depression. I had spent my life agonizing over my origins. Now the old man's words seemed to lodge in my ear. My father had schooled me in the old religion which said that Master and

Servant was the way of the universe and that final Enlightenment was to embrace one's Master and one's death simultaneously. It is what we waited for, this symmetry, and it informed our lives, was the north star that we followed.

My father was a devout man, but I was losing my faith, as though the old man's words had cracked the container of doubt, and doubt now irradiated every thought. Perhaps we were from outer space and so long lost to our purpose, so profoundly out of sync, that we had lost our minds.

The thought that I might be insane drove me, perversely, to insane acts. Behind the estate lay acres of forest and meadow. I would walk in the fields at night. I would dig deep holes in the ground and lie down and scrape the sweet and cloying earth over me and think: "I am dead." And I would lie there without breathing. Once a wild and sudden thunderstorm broke over my self-made grave, and a great deal of mud and water found its way into my lungs, and my voice, for two days, popped and gurgled like a stew on the boil.

I was not so lost to the world that I failed to perform my duties or in any way indicated what a tentative grip I had on my reason. You, Elaine, might have noticed, might have suspected that I was unraveling, but our afternoon teas were a thing of the past. School and a host of commitments, both social and academic, occupied all your time. I saw you only as a sort of vision, rushing by, arms laden with books, hair now an alarming mass of dark coils that framed your face.

I have not made short work of this letter, and I apologize. Perhaps I have been intentionally delaying the bad news. I am loath to be the instrument of your unhappiness. Your father has returned to drinking. I had feared something might have happened when I learned—from our gardener Clive who also does some work for the Hartleys and gathers a substantial crop of gossip from their housekeeper—that Miss Kelly had abruptly shifted affections, and her heart now resided in the care of a young systems analyst.

Your father remained sober and unaffected, and I decided that I had overestimated the extent of his heart's commitment to Miss Kelly. Perhaps he was glad to see the last of her. She did, as you have noted, have a pronounced overbite and a jarring sort of laugh such as a torturer might elicit. Perhaps he had ceased seeing her and she had quickly found another.

And then your father was drunk and his apparent indifference was revealed as simple shock and a vain denial of the truth.

I am afraid his rages are worse than ever. Remember that Chinese vase that you so despised? Well, you needn't despise it any more; it is smashed. So are several televisions, the hall mirror, four windows. Natalie is quite exhausted cleaning up.

I fear that that is not the worst of it. Three nights ago I was awakened at two in the morning by groans of a particularly pathetic nature, and I approached the open study door and peered into the room. Your father's back was to me and he was studying a series of Polaroids that lay on the desk in front of him. My eyesight is exceptionally acute, but from my vantage point I could make out no more than their general content: a man and a woman, nude, were engaged in various sexual acts.

Your father must have sensed my presence, for he turned abruptly and gestured violently for me to enter the room. "Take a good look and damn her!" he shouted. I looked then, expecting to see Miss Kelly and her systems analyst, compromised by a private detective's sordid photos. Instead, I blinked at your impish grin inspired by the X-rated embrace of your lover. I recognized the young man as one you had brought to the house several times in the fall, a well-groomed, athletic, and somewhat inarticulate man who had never seemed a real contender for your heart. In any event, you both seemed to be enjoying yourselves, smirking at the self-timed Polaroid and endeavoring not to topple over before the flash was triggered and your adolescent erotica was captured on film. I regret having to inform you that I saw those photos—knowing that you retained them in privacy and that my knowledge of them can only bring you embarrassment and shame. I can assure you, for what it is worth, that I found the photos not the least bit repellant or obscene, but rather the natural expression of youthful high spirits, and really quite endearing. I am not a prude, and sex has always seemed to me the manifestation of life's exuberance.

Your father told me he had found the photos in an envelope taped to the back of your dresser. His reaction has been, I am afraid, extreme. Indeed, he seems less like an outraged parent and more like an outraged lover. I believe his mind, confused by drink and the recent desertion of Miss Kelly, has taken this last discovery as a massive and demonic betrayal. He is often incoherent as he rages through the rooms. When I can make out his words, they invariably refer to woman's infidelity and treachery.

You and I are both aware of your father's violent nature, and I believe he is awaiting your arrival. Spring break, I understand, is less than two weeks away.

One last development. The fears I have expressed for my own sanity seem warranted. I have spent much time underground, and a certain absentmindedness assails me. I neglect my duties and forget to clean up. My hair is often matted with the mud of my interment. My coat pockets are full of leaves and—on a humorous note—I discovered a field mouse in my trouser cuff. Without thinking I crushed it and caught the dripping blood in my mouth. I'm afraid Natalie saw me do this, and she has since exhibited a certain coolness in my company. In fact, I believe she has left the premises along with the rest of the staff. Your father and I remain, neither of us in the best of mental health.

There is hope, however. Yesterday your father, exhausted, stared at me—he seems to find nothing remarkable in my appearance—and said, "Life is hard, Jeeves." This is very close to the proper phrasing. There are over two hundred codified ways in which he can phrase it. Should he speak any one of them, should he suggest that he is tired of life and wishes to be relieved of it, then I am at liberty to exercise my Servanthood.

The late Mr. Tate said, "I wish I could sleep forever," a statement which satisfied all the requirements and allowed my father to act in accordance with our Law. I await the same blessing, the same call to Merge. I have every confidence that your father, in his despair, will accommodate me.

In any event, it should be clear that your homecoming, while anticipated, could have tragic consequences. I am told that many students take this respite from their studies as an opportunity to frequent the neighboring beaches. I thought you might enjoy following their example, and upon your return to college the situation will, I trust, have resolved itself.

Again, I apologize for this presumptuous and troubling correspondence.

Your loving Jeeves,
Harold Brawley

P.S. I have enclosed money for your trip to the beach. I apologize for the soiled condition of these bills, but the box in which they were buried was destroyed by black beetles, strange beetles that make a shrill, rusty noise and taste vaguely metallic.

The Foster Child

1

I came, the hope of my tribe, to the City of Absolutes, in the year of the zero plus two big and a nine. I sought Lena, the girl I had dreamed of as my fingers grew back and I drifted in the waters of Nagoda.

They had killed us long and hard, and scattered what was killed, and howled long prayers over our heads so that, even dead, we grew demoralized and let the enduring truth leak from our essence, as blood leaks from the sky-cracked hands of our prophets.

Had the rivers been less vigilant, we would have blown away, without the strength to even add a voice to the black wind. But the mother rivers caught us and carried us down to Nagoda, just enough of us to make this one, and I call myself Yeats, after a singer from the north who abandoned the name to walk naked through the Country of Dead Trees.

At the gates of the city, I was halted.

I dissembled, saying, "I am a trader from Magoth. I bring gold to trade for machine thoughts wrought by your high engineers in the Temple of Bytes."

"Give us some of your gold," they said, "and we will let you pass."

This I did, but then, being imperfect, I killed them anyway, and separated their limbs from their bodies, according to custom.

I should not have done this. Now they knew I was in the city, and their servants would seek me.

I went immediately to the Garden of News and lay down in a rented coma. There the voice visited me.

"What do you need to know, my son?"

"Oh holy Network," I cried. "I need to know why it must go on, why this getting and spending? The stillness between the stars is our true delight and peace."

"We thought you all were killed," the Network said. "We thought the Void of Incoherence had claimed you and all your generations."

"No," I said. "I am alive and seeking one, Lena by name."

"Why?"

"Love. Implacable love. The line across which life leaps. She is our hope. She will restore our order."

"Flee this place," the Network said. "They come now, flying down the infrastructure."

The spiky shivers told me of their presence. Charred electrons, blue halitosis of ghost robots withered the stale air of the coma. I broke out, wires flapping, and ran down the Street of Philosophers.

I fled inward to the Reference Jungle at the edge of my enemy's lair. I wandered amid ancient paper runes and ragged scholars, one of whom recognized me.

"I fall at your feet," the old man said. "I humble myself, grovel, delete all dignity, that you might grant me a boon."

"Be quick," I said. "I am harried by circumstance."

"One question answered," the old man said, "no more. I have spent my life in worship of knowledge. Tell me, have I been wrong to do this?"

"Yes."

The man looked stricken, as though skewered by revelation. I moved on, into the Field of Arguments where my kind had once chosen to abide and where the greatest of us, Meta, had wounded the Earth and sought his own death, devoured by his students.

I came to the Wall of Congruity, beyond which the wizard Nulson, misshapen, robbed of humanness, did nothing now but covet. And I knew that there I would find Lena, no more than a child.

I reached out and grasped the holohand that extended from the door. Cold ghosts rushed through me and stirred a thousand thousand memories.

"You are not dead, then," the voice said. "It is just as well. I am bored and sick of killing things that hold their lives no tighter than an infant holds a spoon. Come in."

"This time you will not kill me, Nulson," I said. My tongue, hampered by my mission, had difficulty speaking the words.

He glittered with laughter. Around the metal bulk of his person, in blue turbulence like small asteroids, a dust of old capacitors, resistors, ICs spun. "You come for the child."

"I come for the child," I said.

"And why?"

Pride made me tall. "Always this question. And who is its author? Even here, in this lamentable darkness, questions lurk. I come to answer them, of course. I come from love."

"Well there she lies, embraced by sleep. Claim her."

He moved aside, and I saw, in his motion, that he had grown much since our last encounter. All manner of things had accrued to him, wires and devices, some rusted, some gleaming still, some oscillating and humming.

I looked beyond him to the clear glass from which Lena's frozen face, pale as desire in an old man's heart, stared with frosted eyes.

Three tentacles spun out, silver, segmented, and as the first fell on my shoulder I drew my sword and swung. Sparks gauded the darkness and seared the air. The second tentacle wrapped thickly round my thigh; the third one girded my waist.

I struck again and my sword shattered. A dull electric current sought to paralyze me—a new trick this—and I fell down. I was pulled, knees skidding across the concrete, toward my hated foe.

"What made you think you could defeat me? What made you think it would be different?"

He drew me to him.

"The last time I died, I learned," I said. "What good is death if some wisdom does not adhere to the dying?"

"What good indeed!" my enemy roared. "Die in vain twice over."

He drew me to the grinding gears, the teeth that processed blood and flesh and bone.

"I learned where the rat hides in his maze," I said, and I spit the homing dart from my mouth, through the latticework of steel, through the one opening, to where that memory of a monkey shape still lodged. Nulson himself, atrophied, sequestered in his cage within the cybernetic monster he had sprouted, screamed—this was a violent poison that boiled the blood—and a great straining and crying out of metal filled my ears, and I toppled sideways amid blue smoke and the buckling thunder of exploding circuits.

I rose amid the rubble and walked to the glass case and found the secret of it and opened it. I kissed Lena on the forehead and studied her frost-glazed eyes.

2

"You may be the best teacher in the world, Mr. Wilson, but I am afraid that you cannot help my child," Mrs. Jamerson said.

The young man put the cup of tea down and regarded the woman. She was pretty, and he could see an echo of the much-photographed child in her, but worry had aged her, and her blue eyes looked beyond him to some repeated tragedy.

"I've read the articles, of course; the media coverage brought her to my attention. And the institution has briefed me thoroughly," he said.

The woman sighed and ran her hands across the fabric of her dress. Such a well-appointed house, such a decorous woman, such sadness. "Yes, there has been much written about Lena," Mrs. Jamerson said. "So many words, as though a million words could explain her, solve her. Words like 'savant.' But Lena is only Lena, only herself."

"Can I see her?"

"I suppose there is no reason you shouldn't." Lena's mother put down her teacup and stood up. "This way, please."

John Wilson followed her down a hallway. They passed a framed photo of Mr. and Mrs. Jamerson, waving from a yacht— the same photo the newspapers had run, the same photo John Wilson had studied just yesterday. *It must be painful to keep it there*, John thought. *An act of deliberate courage, perhaps.*

Less than a week after that photo was taken, the yacht had been destroyed in a storm. Lena Jamerson—two years old—had fallen into the ocean, and her father had lost his life trying to save her. Lena had survived, but near drowning, oxygen deprivation, had done some damage. She was not the same. And it was this alteration that drew the newspapers, always hungry for the unique, the bizarre, the uncanny.

"Lena," Mrs. Jamerson said, ushering John Wilson into the room. "I've brought you a visitor."

The room was decorated with posters of animals. Sunlight streamed through a window, falling on a doll that sat crookedly in a small white chair.

A little girl, dressed in a blue smock with white knee-length socks and white tennis shoes, sat cross-legged on a canopied bed. Her hair was pale blond, almost white, and combed to a sunstruck luster. She was staring straight in front of her and her eyes were the blue one encounters when breaking the ocean's surface after diving off a boat somewhere in the Caribbean.

"She has always been the most beautiful girl in the world," her mother said, speaking from behind him. "There is nothing about Lena that is not extraordinary. You know, as a baby, she did nothing but laugh, I believe, on occasion, I heard her giggle when I was carrying her, months before her birth."

"She is a princess," Wilson said. She was like a china figurine, an enchanted fairy.

"She does not relate to the world around her. She is amused but passive. She smiles often, laughs, but she is unaware of our presence. She can feed herself. She is toilet trained. Oh, in many respects, she is the model child. But she sleepwalks through her life." Lena's mother walked to the bed, sat down, and put her arms around her daughter, who continued to stare straight ahead, hands primly nested in her lap.

"A year ago, at the age of five, she spoke. My sister and I were at the breakfast table. Lena said, 'Thou still unravished bride of quietness, thou foster-child of silence and slow time.'"

Wilson nodded. "Keats. The beginning of 'Ode on a Grecian Urn.'"

"Hardly 'Mommy,'" Lena's mother said. "Those were the first words she ever uttered. My sister is a professor of English literature—as the more skeptical reporters noted immediately—and she recognized the quote. But I assure you, as I have assured a horde of doubters, that we did not coach her. Since then any number of investigators, including some from the institution with which you are affiliated, Mr. Wilson, have satisfied themselves that Lena speaks only in fragments of poetry and that she ranges across all nationalities and times. If you are yet another man determined to expose a fraud, you are doomed to failure. Lena does not read; she has not been exposed to these poets. This is not a 'savant' syndrome; Lena is not one of those children with greatly impaired mental faculties who can mimic classical piano pieces after one listening. In Lena's case, there is no source to mimic."

"Yes," he said, "It is incredible."

The first touch of anger darkened his hostess's voice. "And how do you explain it?"

"Well. I'm not sure that anyone can explain it. It is mysterious."

"Then you haven't given it sufficient thought, Mr. Wilson. Your institution should have asked a poet. Any poet could have told them that Lena simply listens to the Muse. She is not quoting William Blake or Shakespeare or Milton or anyone else. My Lena is listening to the source of all inspiration. The Muse is dictating to her directly. Don't poets say their visions come from some mysterious otherworld? Well, my poor Lena has been shouted deaf by that mystery voice, that voice poets call the Muse."

Lena's mother drew the child to her and hugged her tightly. Eyes wet now, emotion in her voice, she addressed Wilson as though the whole of science, in all its vanity, stood before her. "You can't do anything for her. You say you are a teacher? Wonderful. Will you teach her to quote 'Dover Beach?' Hah! Better if you can teach her how to poison this Muse. Teach her how to kill the voice within her. Teach her how to return to her mother and her aunt, to hear our unrhymed voices that love her and call her name every day, and get no answer and watch our beautiful child drift further and further from us."

"I understand your feelings," Wilson said. "But, without wishing to raise false hopes, I think I might be able to help. People...people talk to me."

Mrs. Jamerson regarded him with a weary smile. She said, "I think you have met your match."

"I would like to come here every day," he said. "I would like to take Lena on some outings, picnics, that sort of thing."

Mrs. Jamerson lifted her child in her arms, stroking the child's bright hair. "You can do no harm, I suppose."

3

The trees had turned to explosive reds, yellows like pennants in a festive football crowd. There was smoke in the autumn air. Lena's mother had dressed Lena warmly, a green sweater, corduroy pants. Wilson held Lena's hand as they stood there on the side of the mountain. It was a sign of Mrs. Jamerson's trust in him that she no longer accompanied them on their outings.

"Are you the leaf, the blossom or the bole!" he quoted. "O body swayed to music, O brightening glance, how can we know the dancer from the dance?" Lena said, completing the quote.

Wilson had learned this trick, so gratifying at first and now, two months later, so frustrating, so heartbreaking. Here was Lena, relating, logically and absolutely, to his voice. Feedback!

He would say, "Light breaks where no sun shines," and Lena would seem to answer, her small voice like a hallelujah choir in his ears: "Where no sea runs, the waters of the heart push in their tides."

So gratified was Wilson that he immediately showed this trick to Mrs. Jamerson, and so he instilled false, cruel hopes. Lena was still remote, a good-humored little ghost, indifferent to her surroundings and to the desperate affection and suffering of those who loved her. He reproached himself now for announcing this parlor trick of triggered quotes as though it were real progress.

Recently he had been plagued by bad dreams. He seemed to be losing a battle with time; a dreadful sense of urgency would suddenly slam him awake at three in the morning. Sweating, suspecting some intruder had invaded his small apartment, he would get up and turn on all the lights and search the entire house, even opening dresser drawers—as though this invading menace might be the size of a rat, a serpent.

Still, it was a beautiful North Carolina autumn and it was a sacrilege to waste it with night-fears and negativity. The poems he knew were English, and many of them too sedate for such a day, but Gerald Manley Hopkins would do. "The world is charged with the grandeur of God," he shouted, lifting Lena and swinging her in a circle.

"It will flame out like shining from shook foil!" Lena shouted back.

For a while he forgot all his failures. They ate their packed lunches under a bright, warming sun. A scattering of crows raced like schoolboys to a recess bell, over the sky and away in a clamor of raucous voices.

4

I had freed her from the wizard Nulson and carried her from the city. Her limbs were still cold, despite the tropical Contested Zone we traveled through, and when I lay in near-death trance, in the House of Solemnity to which I had brought the child, I found the door of her mind swung open on an empty room. She had tired of her imprisonment, and she had leapt recklessly toward the abyss. She had neglected the memory pinions; the cables of desire had been cast off, and so she spun away like a kite that snaps its string, unmoored and beyond all returning.

I screamed awake, breaking the circuits of trance-net with such ferocity that small flames ignited in the encumbering sheets.

"Gone!" I screamed. "Lost!"

My host, Portheria, reprimanded me: "Please, less despair," she urged. "My kin-shepherds are sensitized to you and your quest. You've bruised many of them."

I apologized to the cowled monks, and, still abstracted, walked to Lena, sleeping in her web, all our new-brood hopes imperiled by her abandonment. "Oh, Queen," I sighed, "We are numb with knowledge. The world is dying in the knowing of things. All the waters of love, of empathy, are drained by tireless, inhuman engines. Children are crushed under the wheels without a whimper, and their parents do not weep. We need your holy compassion. Only compassion and love can save us. Just yesterday Volander Inc. merged with Welger Limited and the acid vats claimed two hundred thousand superfluous employees."

The dream child said nothing. Portheria touched my shoulder.

"Despair perhaps later," she said. Her words were always awkward in the air, but she was the greatest empath in the empire, and so her thoughts cut with clarity into my troubled mind. "My kin-shepherds and I can find her yet. We will task our energies to all limits."

"The universes are so wide," I said, unwilling to rise to the bait of hope.

"We will weave a great net of words," Portheria said. We will fish for her in all the languages of dreams, down all the years, with all the love and sorrow that she must hunger for."

And so I retired apart from them, prepared for a wait of some years—knowing that our world unraveled at a quicker pace.

5

"You are a stubborn young man," Mrs. Jamerson said, speaking into the phone. "But I think there is some virtue in acceptance. It is time to admit that Lena has defeated you. She remains aloof and alone, my impossible child."

John Wilson had come to know Mrs. Jamerson well. He marveled at the woman's courage, and felt a genuine, ever-growing affection.

"I want to come by tomorrow around noon and take Lena to meet a friend of mine," Wilson said.

Mrs. Jamerson sighed. "Another scientist, I suppose. Another student of the mind. Oh John, let it go."

"I want Lena to meet Sara Palliser. Sara has won a Pulitzer Prize, so you might be familiar with the name. She is a poet."

"What do you hope to accomplish, John?"

"Mrs. Jamerson," John Wilson said, "probably nothing. But I remembered something you said. You said that Lena doesn't quote the poetry of individual poets. She goes to the Muse, the Source of inspiration, and there finds the same poems that have bloomed in the hearts and minds of our great bards. So...suppose...Sara Palliser is a friend of mine. I had lunch with her yesterday, and she spoke of an unfinished poem. She said to me, 'It is not really unfinished. Somewhere it is complete. I just have to unearth the rest of it.' And I thought—it burst upon me—that Lena would know where the rest of the poem was. If she and Sara...well, you see, if they could go there together, if they made the journey at the same time under hypnosis—Dr. Byrne at the institution would serve as a guide—then they could talk to one another. Sara Palliser could speak to Lena. Lena could answer."

"John—"

"Tomorrow at noon. See you then." John Wilson hung up.

6

I was awakened from a deep slumber. The whisper moths that had been drawn by my dreams fluttered away to drift in a pink cloud high above my head.

"We have found her," Portheria said. There was an anxiety in her tone that should not have accompanied such news.

"What is wrong? What year is it?"

"We've found her soon enough," said Portheria, anticipating my fear. "But you must act immediately. There is one there, well-intentioned but ignorant of the forces at risk, who is prepared to draw her into the new world she inhabits. He has found a singer who—we all agree—can awaken her. Once awakened to her new home, she will be lost to us forever."

"I go then," I said. "Show me the quadrant and I will surrender my will to your soul-steering."

7

Wilson could not sleep that night. He got up and turned the radio on. A flurry of static crackled in the cold night of the apartment and then an organ-voiced version of "Silent Night" flared to sudden clarity. He had forgotten that Christmas was only a week away. He would have to buy presents for his parents, his sister, a few friends.

Wilson went to turn the radio off—the music of the season somehow saddened him—but then another burst of static, and a voice, or no voice at all but something like an articulate wind, said, "That is no country for old men."

And Wilson slept late the next morning, and awoke feeling sluggish and thinking that this dullness heralded the beginning of a cold.

And as he drove over to see Mrs. Jamerson and fetch her daughter, a few large flakes of snow spiraled down from an overly bright sky.

Mrs. Jamerson greeted him at the door. She threw her arms around him. "I've talked to Lena," she said.

She began to cry, sobbing against Wilson's shoulder. "If she can live there whole, then she must go there of course."

"I don't understand," Wilson said. "Just what did she say? How did it come about?"

Wilson stopped. A black bird perched on the sofa arm next to Lena. Lena raised her head, and instantly Wilson saw recognition, felt his heart reverberate as though some vast, inaudible chord resounded within.

"Say the words, John Wilson," Lena urged.

He spoke them as though born with them, suddenly savant himself. He knew then, that this was the last poem they would share.

"That is no country for old men," he began.

"...therefore I have sailed the seas and come to the holy city of Byzantium," Lena said, her words enlivened by the fire in her blue eyes.

I know what's coming, John Wilson thought.

Her last words were whispered, "...of what is past, or passing, or to come."

"Goodbye, Mother. Goodbye, John Wilson," she said. Her image had already begun to fade.

The nightingale hopped to the child's shoulder where it too dimmed.

Mrs. Jamerson spoke from behind Wilson. "There is nothing about Lena that is not extraordinary," she said, pride trembling in her voice. "They bow down to her in Byzantium."

The Halfway House
at the
Heart of Darkness

*K*eel wore a ragged shirt with the holo *Veed There, Simmed That* shimmering on it. She wore it in and out of the virtual. If she was in an interactive virtual, the other players sometimes complained. Amid the dragons and elves and swords of fire, a bramble-haired girl, obviously spiking her virtual with drugs and refusing to tune her shirt to something suitably medieval, could be distracting.

"Fizz off," Keel would say, in response to all complaints.

Keel was difficult. Rich, self-destructive, beautiful, she was twenty years old and already a case study in virtual psychosis.

She had been rehabbed six times. She could have died that time on Makor when she went blank in the desert. She still bore the teeth marks of the land eels that were gnawing on her shoulder when they found her.

A close one. You can't revive the digested.

No one had to tell Keel that she was in rehab again. She was staring at a green ocean, huge white clouds overhead, white gulls filling the heated air with their cries.

131

They gave you these serenity mock-ups when they were bringing you around. They were fairly insipid and several shouts behind the technology. This particular V-run was embarrassing. The ocean wasn't continuous, probably a seven-minute repeat, and the sun's heat was patchy on her face.

The beach was empty. She was propped up in a lounge chair—no doubt her position back in the ward. With concentration, focusing on her spine, she could sense the actual contours of the bed, the satiny feel of the sensor pad.

It was work, this focusing, and she let it go. Always better to flow.

Far to her right, she spied a solitary figure. The figure was moving toward her.

It was, she knew, a wilson. She was familiar with the drill. Don't spook the patient. Approach her slowly after she is sedated and in a quiet setting.

The wilson was a fat man in a white suit (*neo-Victorian, dead silly*, Keel thought). He kept his panama hat from taking flight in the wind by clamping it onto his head with his right hand and leaning forward.

Keel recognized him. She even remembered his name, but then it was the kind of name you'd remember: Dr. Max Marx.

He had been her counselor, her wilson, the last time she'd crashed. Which meant she was in Addiction Resources Limited, which was located just outside of New Vegas.

Dr. Marx looked up, waved, and came on again with new purpose.

A pool of sadness welled in her throat. There was nothing like help, and its pale sister hope, to fill Keel's soul with black water.

Fortunately, Dr. Max Marx wasn't one of the hearty ones. The hearty ones were the worst. Marx was, in fact, refreshingly gloomy, his thick black beard and eyebrows creating a doomed stoic's countenance.

"Yes," he said, in response to her criticism of the virtual, "this is a very miserable effect. You should see the sand crabs. They are laughable, like toys." He eased himself down on the sand next to her and took his hat off and fanned it in front of his face. "I apologize. It must be very painful, a connoisseur of the vee like you, to endure this."

Keel remembered that Dr. Marx spoke in a manner subject to interpretation. His words always held a potential for sarcasm.

"We are portable," Dr. Marx said. "We are in a mobile unit, and so, alas, we don't have the powerful stationary AdRes equipment at our command. Even so, we could do better, there are better mock-ups to be had, but we are not prospering these days. Financially, it has been a year of setbacks, and we have had to settle for some second-rate stuff."

"I'm not in a hospital?" Keel asked.

Marx shook his head. "No. No hospital."

Keel frowned. Marx, sensing her confusion, put his hat back on his head and studied her through narrowed eyes. "We are on the run, Keel Benning. You have not been following the news, being otherwise occupied, but companies like your beloved Virtvana have won a major legislative battle. They are now empowered to maintain their customer base aggressively. I believe the wording is 'protecting customer assets against invasive alienation by third-party services.' Virtvana can come and get you."

Keel blinked at Dr. Marx's dark countenance. "You can't seriously think someone would...what?...kidnap me?"

Dr. Marx shrugged. "Virtvana might. For the precedent. You're a good customer."

"Vee moguls are going to sweat the loss of one spike? That's crazy."

Dr. Marx sighed, stood up, whacked sand from his trousers with his hands. "You noticed then? That's good. Being able to recognize crazy, that is a good sign. It means there is hope for your own sanity."

Her days were spent at the edge of the second-rate ocean. She longed for something that would silence the Need. She would have settled for a primitive bird-in-flight simulation. Anything. Some corny sex-with-dolphins loop— or something abstract, the color red leaking into blue, enhanced with aural-D.

She would have given ten years of her life for a game of Apes and Angels, Virtvana's most popular package. Apes and Angels wasn't just another smooth metaphysical mix—it was the true religion to its fans. A gamer started out down in the muck on Libido Island, where the senses were indulged with perfect, shimmerless sims. Not bad, Libido Island, and some gamers stayed there a long, long time. But what put Apes and Angels above the best pleasure pops was this: A player could *evolve spiritually*. If you followed the Path, if you were steadfast, you became more compassionate, more aware, at one with the universe...all of which was accompanied by feelings of euphoria.

Keel would have settled for a legal rig. Apes and Angels was a chemically enhanced virtual, and the gear that true believers wore was stripped of most safeguards, tuned to a higher reality.

It was one of these hot pads that had landed Keel in Addiction Resources again.

"It's the street stuff that gets you in trouble," Keel said. "I've just got to stay clear of that."

"You said that last time," the wilson said. "You almost died, you know."

Keel felt suddenly hollowed, beaten. "Maybe I want to die," she said.

Dr. Marx shrugged. Several translucent seagulls appeared, hovered over him, and then winked out. "Bah," he muttered. "Bad therapy-V, bad death-wishing clients, bad career choice. Who doesn't want to die? And who doesn't get that wish, sooner or later?"

One day, Dr. Marx said, "You are ready for swimming."

It was morning, full of a phony, golden light. The nights were black and dreamless, nothing, and the days that grew out of them were pale and untaxing. It was an intentionally bland virtual, its sameness designed for healing.

Keel was wearing a one-piece white bathing suit. Her counselor wore bathing trunks, baggy with thick black vertical stripes; he looked particularly solemn, in an effort, no doubt, to counteract the farcical elements of rotund belly and sticklike legs.

Keel sighed. She knew better than to protest. This was necessary. She took her wilson's proffered hand, and they walked down to the water's edge. The sand changed from white to gray where the water rolled over it, and they stepped forward into the salt-smelling foam.

Her legs felt cold when the water enclosed them. The wetness was now more than virtual. As she leaned forward and kicked, her muscles, taut and frayed, howled.

She knew the machines were exercising her now. Somewhere her real body, emaciated from long neglect, was swimming in a six-foot aquarium whose heavy seas circulated to create a kind of liquid treadmill. Her lungs ached; her shoulders twisted into monstrous knots of pain.

In the evening, they would talk, sitting in their chairs and watching the ocean swallow the sun, the clouds turning orange, the sky occasionally spotting badly, some sort of pixel fatigue.

"If human beings are the universe's way of looking at itself," Dr. Marx said, "then virtual reality is the universe's way of pretending to look at itself."

"You wilsons are all so down on virtual reality," Keel said. "But maybe it is the natural evolution of perception. I mean, everything we see is a product of the equipment we see it with. Biological, mechanical, whatever."

Dr. Marx snorted. "Bah. The old 'everything-is-virtual' argument. I am ashamed of you, Keel Benning. Something more original, please. We wilsons are down on virtual addiction because everywhere we look we see dead philosophers. We see them and they don't look so good. We smell them, and they stink. That is our perception, our primitive reality."

The healing was slow, and the sameness, the boredom, was a hole to be filled with words. Keel talked, again, about the death of her parents and her brother. They had been over this ground the last time she'd been in treatment, but she was here again, and so it was said again.

"I'm rich because they are dead," she said.

It was true, of course, and Dr. Marx merely nodded, staring in front of him. Her father had been a wealthy man, and he and his young wife and Keel's brother, Calder, had died in a freak air-docking accident while vacationing at Keypond Terraforms. A "sole survivor" clause in her father's life insurance policy had left Keel a vast sum.

She had been eleven at the time—and would have died with her family had she not been sulking that day, refusing to leave the hotel suite.

She knew she was not responsible, of course. But it was not an event you wished to dwell on. You looked, naturally, for powerful distractions.

"It is a good excuse for your addiction," Dr. Marx said. "If you die, maybe God will say, 'I don't blame you.' Or maybe

God will say, 'Get real. Life's hard.' I don't know. Addiction is in the present, not the past. It's the addiction itself that leads to more addictive behavior."

Keel had heard all this before. She barely heard it this time. The weariness of the evening was real, brought on by the day's physical exertions. She spoke in a kind of woozy, presleep fog, finding no power in her words, no emotional release.

Of more interest were her counselor's words. He spoke with rare candor, the result, perhaps, of their fugitive status, their isolation.

It was after a long silence that he said, "To tell you the truth, I'm thinking of getting out of the addiction treatment business. I'm sick of being on the losing side."

Keel felt a coldness in her then, which, later, she identified as fear.

He continued: "They are winning. Virtvana, MindSlide, Right to Flight. They've got the sex, the style, and the flash. All we wilsons have is a sense of mission, this knowledge that people are dying, and the ones that don't die are being lost to lives of purpose.

"Maybe we're right—sure, we're right—but we can't sell it. In two, three days we'll come to our destination and you'll have to come into Big R and meet your fellow addicts. You won't be impressed. It's a henry-hovel in the Slash. It's not a terrific advertisement for Big R."

Keel felt strange, comforting her wilson. Nonetheless, she reached forward and touched his bare shoulder. "You want to help people. That is a good and noble impulse."

He looked up at her, a curious nakedness in his eyes. "Maybe that is hubris."

"Hubris?"

"Are you not familiar with the word? It means to try to steal the work of the gods."

Keel thought about that in the brief moment between the dimming of the seascape and the nothingness of night.

She thought it would be a fine thing to do, to steal the work of the gods.

Dr. Marx checked the perimeter, the security net. All seemed to be in order. The air was heavy with moisture and the cloying odor of mint. This mint scent was the olfactory love song of an insect-like creature that flourished in the tropical belt. The creature looked like an unpleasant mix of spider and wasp. Knowing that the sweet scent came from it, Dr. Marx breathed shallowly and had to fight against an inclination to gag. Interesting, the way knowledge affected one. An odor, pleasant in itself, could induce nausea when its source was identified.

He was too weary to pursue the thought. He returned to the mobile unit, climbed in and locked the door behind him. He walked down the corridor, paused to peer into the room where Keel rested, sedated electrically.

He should not have spoken his doubts. He was weary, depressed, and it was true that he might very well abandon this crumbling profession. But he had no right to be so self-revealing to a client. As long as he was employed, it behooved him to conduct himself in a professional manner.

Keel's head rested quietly on the pillow. Behind her, on the green panels, her heart and lungs created cool, luminous graphics. Physically, she was restored. Emotionally, mentally, spiritually, she might be damaged beyond repair.

He turned away from the window and walked on down the corridor. He walked past his sleeping quarters to the control room. He undressed and lay down on the utilitarian flat and let the neuronet embrace him. He was aware, as always, of guilt and a hangdog sense of betrayal.

The virtual had come on the Highway two weeks ago. He'd already left Addiction Resources with Keel, traveling west into the wilderness of Pit Finitum, away from the treatment center and New Vegas.

Know the enemy. He'd sampled all the vees, played at lowest res with all the safeguards maxed, so that he could talk knowledgeably with his clients. But he'd never heard of this virtual—and it had a special fascination for him. It was called *Halfway House.*

A training vee, not a recreational one, it consisted of a series of step-motivated, instructional virtuals designed to teach the apprentice addictions counselor his trade.

So why this guilt attached to methodically running the course?

What guilt?

That guilt.

Okay. Well…

The answer was simple enough: Here all interventions came to a good end, all problems were resolved, all clients were healed.

So far he had intervened on a fourteen-year-old boy addicted to Clawhammer Comix, masterfully diagnosed a woman suffering from Leary's syndrome, and led an entire group of mix-feeders through a nasty withdrawal episode.

He could tell himself he was learning valuable healing techniques.

Or he could tell himself that he was succumbing to the world that killed his clients, the hurt-free world where everything worked out for the best, good triumphed, bad withered and died, rewards came effortlessly—and if that was not enough, the volume could always be turned up.

He had reservations. Adjusting the neuronet, he thought, "I will be careful." It was what his clients always said.

Keel watched the insipid ocean, waited. Generally, Dr. Marx arrived soon after the darkness of sleep had fled. He did not come at all. When the sun was high in the sky, she began to shout for him. That was useless, of course.

She ran into the ocean, but it was a low res ghost and only filled her with vee-panic. She stumbled back to the beach chair, tried to calm herself with a rational voice: *Someone will come.*

But would they? She was, according to her wilson, in the wilds of Pit Finitum, hundreds of miles to the west of New Vegas, traveling toward a halfway house hidden in some dirty corner of the mining warren known as the Slash.

Darkness came, and the programmed current took her into unconsciousness.

The second day was the same, although she sensed a physical weakness that emanated from Big R. Probably nutrients in one of the IV pockets had been depleted. *I'll die*, she thought. Night snuffed the thought.

A new dawn arrived without Dr. Marx. Was he dead? And if so, was he dead by accident or design? And if by design, whose? Perhaps he had killed himself; perhaps this whole business of Virtvana's persecution was a delusion.

Keel remembered the wilson's despair, felt a sudden conviction that Dr. Marx had fled Addiction Resources without that center's knowledge, a victim of the evangelism/paranoia psychosis that sometimes accompanied counselor burnout.

Keel had survived much in her twenty years. She had donned some deadly v-gear and made it back to Big R intact. True, she had been saved a couple of times, and she probably wasn't what anyone would call psychologically sound, but…it would be an ugly irony if it was an addictions rehab, an unhinged wilson, that finally killed her.

Keel hated irony, and it was this disgust that pressed her into action.

She went looking for the plug. She began by focusing on her spine, the patches, the slightly off-body temp of the sensor pad. Had her v-universe been more engrossing, this would have been harder to do, but the ocean was deteriorating daily, the seagulls now no more than scissoring disruptions in the mottled sky.

On the third afternoon of her imposed solitude, she was able to sit upright in Big R. It required all her strength, the double-think of real Big-R motion while in the virtual. The affect in vee was to momentarily tilt the ocean and cause the sky to leak blue pixels into the sand.

Had her arms been locked, had her body been glove-secured, it would have been wasted effort, of course, but Keel's willing participation in her treatment, her daily exercise regimen, had allowed relaxed physical inhibitors. There had been no reason for Dr. Marx to anticipate Keel's attempting a Big-R disruption.

She certainly didn't want to.

The nausea and terror induced by contrary motion in Big R while simulating a virtual was considerable.

Keel relied on gravity, shifting, leaning to the right. The bed shifted to regain balance.

She screamed, twisted, hurled herself sideways into Big R.

And her world exploded. The ocean raced up the beach, a black tidal wave that screeched and rattled as though some monstrous mechanical beast were being demolished by giant pistons.

Black water engulfed her. She coughed and it filled her lungs. She flayed; her right fist slammed painfully against the side of the container, making it hum.

She clambered out of the exercise vat, placed conveniently next to the bed, stumbled, and sprawled on the floor in naked triumph.

"Hello, Big R," she said, tasting blood on her lips.

Dr. Marx had let the system ease him back into Big R. The sessions room dimmed to glittering black, then the light returned. He was back in the bright control room. He removed the neuronet, swung his legs to the side of the flatbed, stretched. It had been a good session. He had learned something about distinguishing (behaviorally) the transitory feedback psychosis called frets from the organic v-disease, Viller's Pathway.

This Halfway House was proving to be a remarkable instructional tool. In retrospect, his fear of its virtual form had been pure superstition. He smiled at his own irrationality.

He would have slept that night in ignorance, but he decided to give the perimeter of his makeshift compound a last security check before retiring.

To that effect, he dressed and went outside.

In the flare of the compound lights, the jungle's purple vegetation looked particularly unpleasant, like the swollen limbs of long-drowned corpses. The usual skittering things made a racket. There was nothing in the area inclined to attack a man, but the planet's evolution hadn't stinted on biting and stinging vermin, and...

And one of the vermin was missing.

He had, as always, been frugal in his breathing, gathering into his lungs as little of the noxious atmosphere as possible. The cloying mint scent never failed to sicken him.

But the odor was gone.

It had been there earlier in the evening, and now it was gone. He stood in jungle night, in the glare of the compound lights, waiting for his brain to process this piece of information, but his brain told him only that the odor had been there and now it was gone.

Still, some knowledge of what this meant was leaking through, creating a roiling fear.

If you knew what to look for, you could find it. No vee was as detailed as nature.

You only had to find one seam, one faint oscillation in a rock, one incongruent shadow.

It was a first-rate sim, and it would have fooled him. But they had had to work fast, fabricating and downloading it, and no one had noted that a nasty alien bug filled the Big-R air with its mating fragrance.

Dr. Marx knew he was still in the vee. That meant, of course, that he had not walked outside at all. He was still lying on the flat. And, thanks to his blessed paranoia, there was a button at the base of the flat, two inches from where his left hand naturally lay. Pushing it would disrupt all current and activate a hypodermic containing twenty cc's of hapotile-4. Hapotile-4 could get the attention of the deepest v-diver. The aftereffects were not pleasant, but, for many v-devotees, there wouldn't have been an "after" without hapotile.

Dr. Marx didn't hesitate. He strained for the Big R, traced the line of his arm, moved. It was there; he found it. Pressed.

Nothing.

Then, out of the jungle, a figure came.

Eight feet tall, carved from black steel, the vee soldier bowed at the waist. Then, standing erect, it spoke: "We deactivated your failsafe before you embarked, Doctor."

"Who are you?" He was not intimidated by this military mockup, the boom of its metal voice, the faint whine of its servos. It was a virtual puppet, of course. Its masters were the thing to fear.

"We are concerned citizens," the soldier said. "We have reason to believe that you are preventing a client of ours, a client-in-good-credit, from satisfying her constitutionally sanctioned appetites."

"Keel Benning came to us of her own free will. Ask her and she will tell you as much."

"We will ask her. And that is not what she will say. She will say, for all the world to hear, that her freedom was compromised by so-called caregivers."

"Leave her alone."

The soldier came closer. It looked up at the dark blanket of the sky. "Too late to leave anyone alone, Doctor. Everyone is in the path of progress. One day we will all live in the vee. It is the natural home of gods."

The sky began to glow as the black giant raised its gleaming arms.

"You act largely out of ignorance," the soldier said. "The godseekers come, and you treat them like aberrations, like madmen burning with sickness. This is because you do not know the virtual yourself. Fearing it, you have confined and studied it. You have refused to taste it, to savor it."

The sky was glowing gold, and figures seemed to move in it, beautiful, winged humanforms.

Virtvana, Marx thought. *Apes and Angels.*

It was his last coherent thought before enlightenment.

"I give you a feast," the soldier roared. And all the denizens of heaven swarmed down, surrounding Dr. Marx with love and compassion and that absolute, impossible distillation of a hundred thousand insights that formed a single, tear-shaped truth: Euphoria.

Keel found she could stand. A couple of days of inaction hadn't entirely destroyed the work of all that exercise. Shakily, she navigated the small room. The room had the sanitized, hospital look she'd grown to know and loathe. If this room followed the general scheme, the shelves over the bed should contain...They did, and Keel donned one of the gray, disposable client suits.

She found Dr. Marx by the noise he was making, a kind of *huh, huh, huh* delivered in a monotonous chant and punctuated by an occasional *Ah!* The sounds, and the writhing, near-naked body that lay on the table emitting these sounds, suggested to Keel that her doctor, naughty man, might be auditing something sexual on the virtual.

But a closer look showed signs of v-overload epilepsy. Keel had seen it before and knew that one's first inclination, to shut down every incoming signal, was not the way to go. First you shut down any chemical enhancers—and, if you happened to have a hospital handy (as she did), you slowed the system more with something like clemadine or hetlin—then, if you were truly fortunate and your spike was epping in a high-tech detox (again, she was so fortunate), you plugged in a regulator, spliced it and started running the signals through that, toning them down.

Keel got to it. As she moved, quickly, confidently, she had time to think that this was something she knew about (a consumer's knowledge, not a tech's, but still, her knowledge was extensive).

Dr. Marx had been freed from the virtual for approximately ten minutes (but was obviously not about to break the surface of Big R), when Keel heard the whine of the security alarm. The front door of the unit was being breached with an L-saw.

Keel scrambled to the corridor where she'd seen the habitat sweep. She swung the ungainly tool around, falling to one knee as she struggled to unbolt the barrel lock. *Fizzing pocky low-tech grubber.*

The barrel-locking casing clattered to the floor just as the door collapsed.

The man in the doorway held a weapon, which, in retrospect, made Keel feel a little better. Had he been weaponless, she would still have done what she did.

She swept him out the door. The sonic blast scattered him across the cleared area, a tumbling, bloody mass of rags and unraveling flesh, a thigh bone tumbling into smaller bits as it rolled under frayed vegetation.

She was standing in the doorway when an explosion rocked the unit and sent her crashing backward. She crawled down the corridor, still lugging the habitat gun, and fell into the doorway of a cluttered storage room. An alarm continued to shriek somewhere.

The mobile now lay on its side. She fired in front of her. The roof rippled and roared, looked like it might hold, and then flapped away like an unholy, howling v-demon, a vast silver blade that smoothly severed the leafy tops of the jungle's tallest sentinels. Keel plunged into the night, ran to the edge of the unit and peered out into the glare of the compound lights.

The man was crossing the clearing.

She crouched, and he turned, sensing motion. He was trained to fire reflexively but he was too late. The rolling sonic blast from Keel's habitat gun swept man and weapon and weapon's discharge into roiling motes that mixed with rock and sand and vegetation, a stew of organic and inorganic matter for the wind to stir.

Keel waited for others to come but none did.

Finally, she reentered the mobile to retrieve her wilson, dragging him (unconscious) into the scuffed arena of the compound.

Later that night, exhausted, she discovered the aircraft that had brought the two men. She hesitated, then decided to destroy it. It would do her no good; it was not a vehicle she could operate, and its continued existence might bring others.

The next morning, Keel's mood improved when she found a pair of boots that almost fit. They were a little tight but, she reasoned, that was probably better than a little loose. They had, according to Dr. Marx, a four-day trek ahead of them.

Dr. Marx was now conscious but fairly insufferable. He could talk about nothing but angels and the Light. A long, hard dose of Apes and Angels had filled him with fuzzy love and an uncomplicated metaphysics in which smiling angels fixed bad stuff and protected all good people (and, it went without saying, all people were good).

Keel had managed to dress Dr. Marx in a suit again, and this restored a professional appearance to the wilson. But, to Keel's dismay, Dr. Marx in virtual-withdrawal was a shameless whiner.

"Please," he would implore. "Please, I am in terrible terrible Neeeeeeed."

He complained that the therapy-v was too weak, that he was sinking into a catatonic state. Later, he would stop entirely, of course, but now, please, something stronger....

No.

He told her she was heartless, cruel, sadistic, vengeful. She was taking revenge for her own treatment program, although, if she would just recall, he had been the soul of gentleness and solicitude.

"You can't be in virtual and make the journey," Keel said. "I need you to navigate. We will take breaks, but I'm afraid they will brief. Say goodbye to your mobile."

She destroyed it with the habitat sweep, and they were on their way. It was a limping, difficult progress, for they took much with them: food, emergency camping and sleeping gear, a portable, two-feed v-rig, the virtual black box, and the security image grabs. And Dr. Marx was not a good traveler.

It took six days to get to the Slash, and then Dr. Marx said he wasn't sure just where the halfway house was.

"What?"

"I don't know. I'm disoriented."

"You'll never be a good v-addict," Keel said. "You can't lie."

"I'm not lying!" Dr. Marx snapped, goggle-eyed with feigned innocence.

Keel knew what was going on. He wanted to give her the slip and find a v-hovel where he could swap good feelings with his old angel buddies. Keel knew.

"I'm not letting you out of my sight," she said.

The Slash was a squalid mining town with every vice a disenfranchised population could buy. It had meaner toys than New Vegas, and no semblance of law.

Keel couldn't just ask around for a treatment house. You could get hurt that way.

But luck was with her. She spied the symbol of a triangle inside a circle on the side of what looked like an abandoned office. She watched a man descend a flight of stairs directly beneath the painted triangle. She followed him.

"Where are we going?" Dr. Marx said. He was still a bundle of tics from angel-deprivation.

Keel didn't answer, just dragged him along. Inside, she saw the "Easy Does It" sign and knew everything was going to be okay.

An old man saw her and waved. Incredibly, he knew her, even knew her name. "Keel," he shouted. "I'm delighted to see you."

"It's a small world, Solly."

"It's that. But you get around some too. You cover some ground, you know. I figured ground might be covering you by now."

Keel laughed. "Yeah." She reached out and touched the old man's arm. "I'm looking for a house," she said.

In Group they couldn't get over it. Dr. Max Marx was a fizzing *client*. This amazed everyone, but two identical twins, Sere and Shona, were so dazed by this event that they insisted on dogging the wilson's every move. They'd flank him, peering into his eyes, trying to fathom this mystery by an act of unrelenting scrutiny.

Brake Madders thought it was a narc thing and wanted to hurt Marx.

"No, he's one of us," Keel said.

And so, Keel thought, *am I.*

When Dr. Max Marx was an old man, one of his favorite occupations was to reminisce. One of his favorite topics was Keel Benning. He gave her credit for saving his life, not only in the jungles of Pit Finitum but during the rocky days that followed when he wanted to flee the halfway house and find, again, virtual nirvana.

She had recognized every denial system and thwarted it with logic. When logic was not enough, she had simply shared his sadness and pain and doubt.

"I've been there," she had said.

The young wilsons and addiction activists knew Keel Benning only as the woman who had fought Virtvana and MindSlip and the vast lobby of Right to Flight, the woman who had secured a resounding victory for addicts' rights and challenged the spurious thinking that suggested a drowning person was drowning by choice. She was a hero, but, like many heroes, she was not, to a newer generation, entirely real.

"I was preoccupied at the time," Dr. Marx would tell young listeners. "I kept making plans to slip out and find some Apes and Angels. You weren't hard pressed then—and you aren't now—to find some mind-flaming vee in the Slash. My thoughts would go that way a lot.

"So I didn't stop and think, 'Here's a woman who's been rehabbed six times; it's not likely she'll stop on the seventh. She's just endured some genuinely nasty events, and she's probably feeling the need for some quality downtime.'

"What I saw was a woman who spent every waking moment working on her recovery. And when she wasn't doing mental, spiritual, or physical push-ups she was helping those around her, all us shaking, vision-hungry, fizz-headed needers.

"I didn't think, 'What the hell is this?' back then. But I thought it later. I thought it when I saw her graduate from medical school."

"When she went back and got a law degree, so she could fight the bastards who wouldn't let her practice addiction medicine properly, I thought it again. That time, I asked her. I asked her what had wrought the change."

Dr. Marx would wait as long as it took for someone to ask, "What did she say?"

"It unsettled me some," he would say, then wait again to be prompted.

They'd prompt.

"'Helping people,' she'd said. She'd found it was a thing she could do, she had a gift for it. All those no-counts and dead-enders in a halfway house in the Slach. She found she could help them all."

Dr. Marx saw it then, and saw it every time after that, every time he'd seen her speaking on some monolith grid at some rally, some hearing, some whatever. Once he'd seen it, he saw it every time: that glint in her eye, the incorrigible, unsinkable addict.

"People," she had said. "What a rush."

The Lights
of Armageddon

The light bulb died with a small pop that scared Mrs. Ward. She was sixty-seven years old, so it wasn't the first time a light bulb had died in her presence. But it was always an unsettling thing. At first, one was apt to think the pop and the world's sudden dimming were internal, as though a brain cell had overexerted itself and suddenly burst.

She was delighted to discover that she was not having a stroke, and, dropping her knitting into her lap, she shouted for her husband.

"What is it, Marge?" he asked, coming up from the basement.

"This lamp blew out," she said.

Her husband walked over to the lamp, unscrewed the bulb, and walked off into the kitchen without saying a word. He returned with a new bulb. "Now we'll see if this sucker works," he said.

"Why shouldn't it work?" Marge asked. Her husband was an exasperating man.

"This is one of those light bulbs you made me buy from that odd fellow come round here yesterday. You remember. He said the money would go to good works and I said, 'What good works?' and he said—and not right away, but like he was making it up—he said, 'The blind.'"

"I remember that you were rude, Harry Ward, and that's

why I had to make you buy a box. Sometimes you act like you were raised by apes."

"I couldn't help laughing," Harry said. "'Light bulbs for the blind is kind of like earplugs for the deaf, ain't it?' I says. Now that was damned funny, but he didn't laugh. And I bought his box of light bulbs, didn't I? Two dozen to a box, Marge!" Harry held the light bulb up and regarded it with narrowed eyes. "Looks okay—which is more than you can say for that fellow hawking them. Here it is, maybe ninety degrees in the shade, and he's got on an overcoat, and his face is as white as plaster and his lips are red—that had to be lipstick, Marge—and he's got a scarf pulled up to his chin like he's freezing."

"The poor man was probably sick, Harry." Marge sighed. Her husband wasn't a sensitive man. He had his good points, of course, but sometimes she was hard pressed to say just what they were. Forty years ago, he had looked good with a mustache, and he had had a kind of haunted, poetic intensity. Now the mustache was gone, and the intensity was a sort of worried, pinched look, like a spinster who's convinced there is a gas leak on the premises.

"I need to get on with this knitting," Marge said.

"Okay," Harry said. "You always were an impatient woman."

Harry leaned over the lamp and screwed the bulb in. The room brightened.

"Well, it works," Harry said.

"Of course it works," Marge said.

Harry went back down into the basement, and Marge returned to her knitting. She dozed off for a while, waking at around ten that evening when Harry came back upstairs.

"I'm going to bed," he said.

"I think I'll read a bit," Marge said. "I'm not the least bit sleepy."

She watched her husband march upstairs. She waited until the bedroom door closed, and then she went into the kitchen. She found the box of light bulbs in a cupboard.

Then she got the stepladder out and placed it in the middle of the floor and climbed up and unscrewed the ceiling light fixture and replaced all three bulbs. She threw the old bulbs in the trash and moved on to the dining room.

By the time she had carried the stepladder upstairs and was unscrewing the light in the bathroom, she was worn out. You never gave a thought to how many light bulbs a house contained until you replaced the lot of them all at once.

And why—why do such a thing? If asked, if stopped by a concerned observer placing a hand on her shoulder, Marge would have said, "Why, I don't know. I can't really say just why." But there was no one to tender the question, and Marge's only thought was that it was a tiresome task. And the bedroom itself would have to wait until morning.

The odd fellow who had sold the light bulbs to the Wards was a magician named Ernest Jones. An accident while conjuring up certain demons had placed him in thrall to the Fair Ones, and he was now doing their bidding, distributing the light bulbs that would call them.

Despite the blazing Florida sun, he was freezing as he worked. He was cold right to the bone, cold clean through.

He was back at the caravan, packing a last light bulb into the box when his rival, a tall, smooth-talking magician named Blake, came into the trailer.

"I know what you are up to," Blake said. "You are lighting the world, so that the Fair Ones may find their way."

"Could be," Jones said. "I would advise you to mind your own business."

"Your advice comes too late," Blake said. "I followed you yesterday. I know what you are up to, and I'm not letting it happen."

"Look," Jones said, turning around. "I tell you what. I'll cut you in. You can be a Vanguard too. The Fair Ones can be quite generous to those who aid them."

Blake, a thin, haughty young man with an imperious air, chuckled. "I am afraid I have already negotiated a different contract. I have made a deal with the Immutable Abyss."

Blake produced a light bulb from his ample magician's pockets. "I have my own beacons," he said.

Jones growled low in his throat and rushed the taller man, who stumbled. The light bulb fell, smashing on the floor. A black, metallic lizard-like creature darted across the linoleum floor, barking sharply.

Jones and Blake wrestled on the floor. Blake suddenly went limp and Jones stood up.

"You sonofabitch," Jones muttered. He began to intone the words that would summon the scavenger demons.

Blake, still lying on the floor, opened his eyes. He produced a small silver revolver and shot Jones in mid-incantation.

Blake summoned his own unholy crew to clean up the corpse. While they were munching on the mortal remains of his rival, Blake methodically destroyed the boxed light bulbs, crushing each spider-like creature as it emerged from its shattered casing. Repacking the box with his Master's own beacons, he sang softly to himself. "That old black magic got me in its spell…"

Louise was new to country living, and she hated it. She was a young woman, twenty-two, in the prime of her life; she wasn't ready to retire to a screened-in porch, a rocking chair, and the conversation of about a jillion insects. Johnny had talked her into moving out here, saying, "I'll be the one who will have to drive fifty miles to work each day. All I'm asking is that you give it a try."

Where had her mind been? she wondered. "Louise Rivers," she said to the empty room, "a siren should go off in your mind when Johnny starts off, 'All I'm asking.'" *All I'm asking is you go to one movie with me. All I'm asking is one kiss.*

All I'm asking is you take off your pantyhose so I can admire your knees. Yeah, sure.

So here she was stuck in the country and it was five miles to the miserable little flyblown grocery store, and no car, and hot enough outside to melt the sunglasses she'd left on the lawn chair.

Louise walked up the dirt road to the Wards, feeling the midday sun breathing on the back of her neck like a rabid dog. The Wards lived in an old farmhouse squatting low in the Florida dust, palmettos flanking the door, a pickup truck under the single live oak tree.

Louise had the grocery list in her hand and the words in her mind: *If you are going to the store, I wonder could you pick up a few things for me.*

The Wards seemed nice enough, an old couple who had been married forever and even looked a bit alike, the way long-married couples will.

Louise knocked on the door. No one answered.

"Hello," Louise called. Maybe they were napping. The country inspired sleep.

Louise knocked louder. She turned the doorknob and pushed. The door swung inward, and an intense flickering light greeted her.

"Mrs. Ward?" Louise shouted. The living room was bathed in silver light that leeched color from the walls, the sofa, the patterned chairs. Mrs. Ward rose from the sofa. The strobe-like flashes made her movements jerky, image superimposed on image.

"Come in, my dear," Mrs. Ward said.

Mrs. Ward took Louise's arm and led her to the sofa.

The room was cold, like being inside a meat locker. Mrs. Ward was wearing several sweaters, and a woolen cap was pulled down over her head, hiding her hair.

Mrs. Ward turned and shouted. "Harry, look who's here. It's our neighbor."

Louise looked to the top of the stairs where Mr. Ward stood. He began to move down the stairs, somewhat awkwardly for he was clasping a large box in his arms.

"Hello, hello!" Mr. Ward shouted. He was smiling and, like his wife, he was bundled up against the cold.

Louise had grown accustomed to the light. The brief moment of terror and dread had passed, and now the light seemed sweetly inquisitive, like the hands of children, shyly touching her face, sliding over her arms, gently stroking her mind.

"It's very bright," Louise said. She had forgotten why she had come.

Mrs. Ward leaned forward and patted Louise's blue-jeaned knee. "Not nearly enough," Mrs. Ward said. "There's not nearly enough light yet. It's still black as night as far as the Fair Ones are concerned. Harry and I do what we can, but we are only two people. You'll help, won't you?"

"Well, of course," said Louise.

Harry shuffled up to them and put the box on the floor. He reached into the box and pulled out a light bulb.

"My dear," Harry said, and he handed it to Louise with a courtly flourish as though presenting a rose.

Louise was charmed. "Why thank you," said Louise. The light bulb was cold and seemed to vibrate when she held it against her cheek.

"Please take a box with you when you go," Mrs. Ward said. "We've plenty."

Country people, thought Louise, *are so generous.*

It was already dark when Johnny took the exit to Polk Hill. He had had to stop once because love bugs had squashed up on the windshield in such numbers that he couldn't see. The Florida travel brochures were curiously silent on these little bastards, who haunted the highways in black clouds, always mating (hence, their name). The rotten insects had created an industry: love bug radiator grille guards, love bug solvent for the windshields, love bug joke bumper stickers.

Still, Johnny loved Florida, the way only a kid from Minnesota can love it. If he never saw another snowfall, another ice-laden tree, it would be okay. Louise had felt the same way. At first they had lived in Tampa but it was too big a city so he had talked Louise into moving out to Polk Hill which was real country, filled with cows and cattle egrets and rednecks with dogs.

Johnny loved it, but Louise was still sort of down on the move. She missed Tampa.

Johnny turned on Waples Drive and slowed to accommodate the much-patched asphalt. Up ahead, light blazed from every window of the Wards' house. *What's the big occasion?* Johnny wondered.

Johnny drove around the curve and saw his own house, light pouring from every window. It was funny how, in the country, lights seemed brighter. He had noticed this before, but it was more pronounced on this moonless night.

Johnny stopped the car and cut the engine.

As he walked along the flagstone steps, he noticed how the light in the windows seemed to pulse. Odd. Looking down he saw that hundreds—thousands—of moths fluttered on the ground. Some of the insects were no bigger than a dime, others quite large with pale green or yellow wings.

Florida did have its share of bugs.

"I wouldn't go in there," a voice said.

Johnny turned to see a tall man wearing a tuxedo, complete with top hat and cape, and sporting a luxuriant handlebar mustache. Next to him was a girl in a sequined bathing suit and high heels.

The man stepped forward. "I'm afraid one of my employees was careless. Jones is a fair magician, but he's no match for any of the third-circle demons, and he was tricked, as easily as you or I might trick a child with a palmed card or a two-sided nickel. Now he has disappeared—consumed, I expect—but the damage has been done."

The man brushed a large moth from his lapel and continued. "I'm Maxwell Kerning, the Amazing Max, and this is my assistant, Doreen. You might have seen the flyers: *Amazing Max and His Traveling WonderRama.* No? Well, it doesn't matter. What does matter is that Jones seems to have recruited your wife and your neighbor in an attempt to summon some unpleasant entities."

"Louise isn't my wife," Johnny said. "We aren't married."

The Amazing Max shrugged his shoulders. "I believe that your precise marital status is incidental to the larger issue—which is the approaching end of civilization."

"I think that is too strong," Doreen said, moving to the magician's side. She had a soft lilting voice, and—Johnny noted—lovely kneecaps. "Probably only Florida would go."

"Disney World would fall," her comrade reminded her. "I believe the destruction of Disney World would pull the plug. Certainly the whole continental nexus would be sucked into that hole. Chaos would reign."

"That's true," Doreen said, her voice even more subdued.

"It's been nice meeting you folks, but I gotta be going," Johnny said. It wasn't good to humor crazy people beyond a certain point. Polite but firm, that was the ticket when interacting with nut cases.

Johnny opened the door to his house and walked into the cold light.

Every light in the house was on, the lot of them flickering like a defective neon sign, and Louise was sitting in the brown armchair. She was wearing an overcoat, wool gloves and earmuffs.

Jesus, Johnny thought. It was colder than Minnesota, and the light reminded him of the curious, ambient glare that filled those northern skies right before a snowstorm. *I don't care for this*, Johnny thought, but even as he thought it some sly, cold hand reached in and stole the thought, scooped it up as though it were a chocolate-covered mint left unattended.

"Hey Louise," Johnny said. "It's sure bright in here."

"It's getting there," Louise said, standing up.

Suddenly Johnny felt his chest being squeezed. He toppled backward and was yanked off his feet. He was dragged out of the room, and the door slammed. The light—the blessed light—was gone and he tried to free his arms and scramble to his feet, his only thought to be reunited with the fierce, cold light.

"Better sit on him for a few minutes while his mind clears," Doreen said.

A terrible headache set in, and Johnny crawled over to a bush and vomited.

"He'll be all right now," he heard the magician say.

Johnny didn't feel like he was apt to rally. He rolled over on his back. A large beetle landed on his forehead, and he brushed it off and sat up. "Jesus." He blinked at Doreen's kneecaps, found some solace there, and asked, "What happened?"

The Amazing Max explained: "Doreen lassoed you. She's an artist with a rope, which I must say is fortunate for you. We almost lost you, you know. I am not a man who enjoys giving advice—let each man find his own path, I say—but you are out of your element here, young man, and I believe you should heed the advice of experienced elders."

Johnny looked at Doreen, who was demurely winding her rope.

"You saved my life," Johnny said.

Doreen looked up and smiled. She had blond, curly hair and black eyes, goggled with eye shadow so she looked a little raccoonian—but sweet.

"I didn't really save your life," Doreen said. "Just maybe your mind."

"Still," Johnny insisted, "I'm beholden."

Doreen fluttered her long eyelashes and looked away.

"I'm Johnny Harmon," Johnny said. "And I won't ever forget it."

The Amazing Max interrupted. "While I am delighted to hear that you will never forget your name, I believe the future in which you remember or forget anything may be brief if we do not address the immediate problem. We've got to pull the switch on all these lights before they attract the Fair Ones."

"Fair Ones?" Johnny asked.

"You don't want to know," the magician said. "Trust me, you don't want to meet them. They'll only have one chance to break through, so they'll wait until the Light is bright enough and then some. I think we've still got time. Where is the fuse box?"

"In the garage," Johnny said.

An investigation revealed the garage door to be down and electronically locked.

The magician questioned Johnny closely, then said, "We'll have to go through the kitchen to get into the garage. Johnny, you'll have to do it. You know the layout. Do you think you can walk through it with your eyes closed?"

"Sure," Johnny said. "The door to the garage is just to the right when you enter the back door."

The magician leaned forward and clutched both of Johnny's shoulders. Amazing Max smelled like cigarettes and Old Spice. "Okay. Now when you get into the garage, don't open your eyes. The light is on there too, I expect. With your eyes closed, can you find the switch for the carport door?" Johnny nodded. "Good. And don't open your eyes until I've said it's okay."

They slipped around to the back of the house, and Johnny unlocked the back door. "Good luck," the magician said, and Johnny, his eyes shut, pushed open the door and entered. He kept his arms out in front of him and he slid his feet forward across the linoleum. He didn't feel the cold like he thought he would, but the darkness behind his eyelids wasn't complete. He could sense the strobe light of the room fluttering on his eyelids; rainbow-hued fragments drifted like ghostfish into his mind.

There were the shelves to his right. China plates, the Abraham Lincoln coffee mug, Louise's antique glass bottle collection…Whoops. A ceramic jug toppled forward and shattered on the floor. It made a loud noise, a sort of *whump-crash* that would have pleased a child. Johnny stood still. The rest of the house was silent.

Keep moving, he told himself. He found the door, felt along the frame until he discovered the doorknob, then turned it. The door swung open.

Woolen fingers touched the back of his neck.

"Ah," Johnny said. Miraculously, he did not open his eyes.

"Hey Johnny," Louise said from behind. "I didn't know what had become of you."

"Just going in the garage here," Johnny mumbled. "Just taking a look in the old garage."

"Well sure," Louise said. She didn't seem intent on stopping him. She wouldn't know that his eyes were closed. Not yet.

Johnny slid his feet across the concrete floor. A can of nails banged over. He almost fell over the extra tire, did in fact lurch forward, arms flaying the air. He regained his balance, found the opposite wall, and began moving toward the carport switch.

Louise spoke again. "What are you doing, Johnny?"

"Just give me a second," Johnny said. "I'll be right back. All I'm asking—"

"Ha!" Louise shouted. She slammed into him from behind, her arms encircling his, hurling him forward. His forehead banged against the wall. But his hand found the switch and he hit it. He heard a clunk sound as the motor engaged, then the metallic rattle and clamor of the door ascending.

"Johnny Harmon!" Louise shouted, but he had turned to embrace her, and he held her tightly as she kicked and raged beneath him. Something exploded, followed by the tinkling sound of glass.

"You can open your eyes now, Johnny," the magician said. "And I might add—well done!"

Johnny opened his eyes in time to see the Amazing Max, a revolver in his hand, stride quickly into the middle of the garage, kick aside the shards of broken glass and, with a satisfied shout, slam a foot down firmly on something that screamed briefly and inhumanly.

It had looked, this now-silenced creature, like a spider, but with the black, shiny, exoskeleton of a beetle.

Johnny staggered to his feet and helped Louise up.

"What was that?" Johnny asked.

"One of the Fair Ones' minions. Not dangerous in themselves, but they are responsible for the light bulbs that call the Fair Ones." The Amazing Max pulled a flashlight from his pocket and turned it on. "Close the garage door again, please."

Johnny hit the switch. The door noisily descended.

They were in darkness now except for the beam of the flashlight.

"I assume that is the fuse box," the magician said. The beam of light played over the grey, rectangular box.

"Yes."

Amazing Max strode to the box, threw the two switches and then, methodically, unscrewed the half dozen fuses and put them in his pocket. "That should do it," he said.

They left the sealed-off garage and entered the now dark-ened house. The flashlight beam played over the kitchen floor, discovering fragments of the shattered jug.

The magician's voice sounded loud in the room. "We'll want to destroy all the light bulbs and look for the queen. She'll be laying more bulbs. Actually, I wouldn't be the least bit surprised if she were right..." The magician threw open the refrigerator door, stepped back and fired into the refrigerator, two blasts that mingled with another inhu-man scream.

"Done then," the magician said. "So far so good."

"How you doing?" Johnny asked, putting an arm around Louise's waist.

"I been better," Louise said. "I'm freezing, for one thing."

They were following the Amazing Max from room to room as he destroyed light bulbs and the creatures within them. It was slow going in the dark, and the screams of the spider-creatures were a little unnerving.

"I reckon you'll warm up in awhile," Johnny said.

The magician, who overheard this remark, said, "No. I'm afraid not." He smashed another bulb, stomped another har-binger of doom.

"What?" Louise said.

The magician was already moving off toward the bed-room, but Louise ran after him, caught his arm, and turned him around. "What do you mean it won't wear off?"

The magician shrugged. "Nothing to wear off, actually. It's a bit of perception shuffling that the light does. The warmer the day, the colder you'll feel. The inverse is true too, so you might consider moving north."

The Amazing Max entered the bedroom and climbed up on the bed. "Hold the flashlight, Doreen," he said, and he began unscrewing the light fixture.

"Well, hell," Louise said. "Goddam hell." She began to sob.

"It will be okay," Johnny said. "We'll keep the air on high or we can move back to Minnesota. We'll think of something."

"Doreen," the magician was saying. "I think that's the lot of them. Fetch those light bulbs from my truck, and we'll begin setting the world right again."

"What about the Wards?" Louise asked.

The Amazing Max walked across the living room and waved an arm at the picture window. "It was too late for the Wards," he said. "They'd gone too far. We had to torch them. We set the incendiary bombs before coming here." Out the window, Johnny could see the guttering flames and an occasional garland of sparks floating into the starless night.

Amazing Max sighed. "I tell you, I'm ready for retirement. First Jones nearly destroys the world, then Blake disappears without a goodbye. I found this in his trailer." Amazing Max pulled a black object from his pocket and handed it to Johnny. It was a grotesque stone lizard-like carving about three inches long.

"What's this?" Johnny asked.

"It's one of the minions of the Immutable Abyss. Deanimated now. The Fair Ones are no picnic, but it looks like Blake was in thrall to even worse news. The Immutable Abyss. Let me tell you"—the magician leaned forward—"you don't even want to think about the kind of things that dwell in the Immutable Abyss."

Max stood up. "Well, let's get going." Amazing Max took the box of light bulbs from Doreen and the tedious task of re-bulbing began.

Louise and Johnny drifted to a sofa.

"I feel awful about the Wards," Louise said. "Plus feeling generally awful."

Johnny nodded. "I guess we should look on the positive side, the end of the world being avoided, that sort of thing."

"I guess so," Louise said.

The magician came back into the living room and plopped into an armchair.

"Another crisis narrowly avoided," he said. He fished in his pocket, took out the fuses. "Doreen," he said. "Would you turn the electricity back on?"

Doreen took the fuses and left the room.

"How was this other magician going to call up the Immutable Abyss?" Johnny asked.

"I have no idea. I can't find him, so I can't ask him." Max shouted. "Hey Doreen! You didn't see Blake today, did you?"

Doreen's voice came back, far away.

"What?"

Max shouted the question again, louder.

"Sure," Doreen shouted back. "I thought I told you. He's the one gave me these light bulbs."

The sun was beginning to come up. Oak trees, cabbage palms, and gaunt pine trees were surfacing in the dishwater dawn. Smoke from the Wards' home rose crookedly into the sky.

The magician was emptying his pockets of the last, unused bulbs. One fell, bursting on the coffee table, and a small, metallic lizard skittered over the mahogany surface, barking mournfully.

"Holy Jesus," the magician croaked. He stood up. "Doreen!" he screamed.

It was too late. The hum of the refrigerator, the thin voice of a radio announcer, the labored wheeze of the air conditioner—all these announced the return of electricity to the household. And of course the lights, the lights went on. They snuffed out the approaching dawn. They emitted a darkness thicker than tar, deeper than black plush velvet lining the inside of a coffin.

Johnny realized that he had never, in fact, encountered darkness. There was the darkness of a moonless night, the darkness of a windowless, midnight room, but this new darkness dwarfed them all. And already, although it could not have been anything but his imagination—many hours would pass before they came—Johnny thought he heard the first thundering footfall.

The Essayist
in the Wilderness

I had won the lottery, the ultimate *deus et machina*.
My wife was stunned by our good fortune, disoriented and faintly miffed for she had always scoffed at my lottery tickets, explaining that a person was more apt to be bitten by a rattlesnake while plummeting to earth in an airplane—"Do the math," she would say—than get that winning number.

I had won, we were rich, and I was very pleased with myself. I could see that Audrey still thought I was dead wrong, that lotteries were the opiate of the people, a game for probability-challenged chumps. However, had events demonstrated the rightness of Audrey's position, we would still be toiling in the English department at Clayton College, a dreary four-year diploma mill with a lovely campus, a mummified faculty, and a student body derived almost entirely from the Church of Christ contingent in certain small towns in Pennsylvania.

We had only settled on Clayton because it offered jobs for the both of us. Audrey had sacrificed the most for that berth. While I taught the glamor stuff, Shakespeare and Spenser and Renaissance poetry, my wife tried to introduce English grammar into the minds of adolescents raised on television and movies—minds that were very nearly immune to syntax.

It didn't take Audrey long to embrace our good fortune. Now we were free. A much smaller sum would have set us free; our desires were modest. We wanted to get away from the infernal ever-busy world, to find a quiet niche where we could read (the unalloyed pleasure of selfish reading, the decadence of perusing books and tossing them aside half read, the dirty thrill of reading novels of no critical merit whatever or old childhood treasures from which the narcotic of nostalgia could be slowly sucked) and, of course, to write.

We bought a house on twenty acres of land in a town beyond the reach of city commuters. We were far from the madding crowd's ignoble strife and spared the reinvented Main Street, the historical markers on every house, the hideous quaintness of the polished past. Our town was a little run down; the unimaginative might even have found it ugly. We loved it.

We lined our rambling, three-story farm house with bookshelves throughout and furnished it with stuff foraged from neighborhood yard sales and junk shops (dressers, mirrors, end tables, a writing desk, a vast old sofa that was as good a representation of Queen Victoria in decline as any sofa I have ever seen).

Once settled, neither of us rushed into writing projects, although Audrey was by far the more industrious. One evening she read me a passage in which her nine-year-old self had accidentally been locked out of the summerhouse in Sag Harbor during a thunderstorm while her parents partied within. She had only been outside a short time, a minute perhaps before her absence was discovered, but it was time enough to get thoroughly wet and abandon a belief system that included loving parents. I thought it was a powerful piece, and I was impressed with the book's tentative title, *Spite*, which struck me as everything a memoir's title should be, forthright, unsparing, monosyllabic.

While I hadn't gotten so far as to conjure a working title or turn any of my thoughts into something as substantial as a paragraph of prose or some lines of poetry, I had spent considerable time deciding just what I intended to write, what genre I would inhabit. As a youth of fourteen, I had wanted to be a lyric poet, but I had failed at that early, discovering that my poetry repelled girls who had initially been drawn to me. In college I considered becoming a novelist, but I was no good at character and if by sheer perseverance I managed to create some sort of fictional personage, I didn't have a clue what to do with him, sending him lurching off down the street like Dr. Frankenstein's monster, inevitably parking him in a cafe or bar where he would talk interminably to some other sadly cobbled-together creature. Nope, not novels. I toyed with the idea of a memoir, but my past bored me. I had no wish to revisit it.

By a process of elimination, I was closing on my vocation. I was reading voraciously, ecstatically, and I had been at it for two months. I expected to find my blushing Muse in the next book that came to hand.

One night we were both reading in the study when I heard a sharp intake of breath and looked up from my book to see Audrey staring wide-eyed in my direction. Her Henry James (*Washington Square* if memory serves) was open on her lap. It was late, about eleven I would guess, and we sat at opposite sides of the room, each of us enclosed in the light of our separate lamps while the books that surrounded us were imbued with dusky mystery and an almost erotic sense of solace.

"Jonathan?" She slapped a hand to her breast as though assaulted by a sudden pain. I assumed she had been taken with some particularly powerful passage and was so expressing herself, for we were both guilty of melodrama in our passion for literature, but then she toppled forward, the book (a Modern Library with those almost transparent pages, those tight thickets of immortal prose) fluttering as she fell.

I marked my place and rushed to her aid. She lay sprawled on the carpet, her flowing blue robe in sweet disarray, her red hair gloriously unbound, as though she were a Victorian heroine felled by the news of her lover's death in a foreign land, the child within her still unknown to the inflexible society of her peers.

I bent down and taking her shoulders lifted her gently, turning her toward me. Did I say that Audrey is beautiful? When I read Jane Austen, I think of my wife, the logic of her cheekbones, the wit of her mouth, her unequivocal eyebrows.

Her eyelids fluttered. "Jonathan?" She seemed incapable of anything else, her mouth open in amazement. Her chest heaved; she gasped. "I can't—I can't breathe."

A series of desperate phone calls revealed that the closest hospital was forty-five miles to the west but that a Dr. Bath would be willing to rouse himself from sleep and meet us at his office at the corner of Maple and Main, a mere five minutes from our home.

A roundish woman swathed in black fabric and wearing a nurse's white cap opened the door before I knocked. She bent forward and clutched Audrey's hand, drawing us both into the room and informing us that she was the doctor's wife. The room was like every doctor's waiting room I have ever seen, a coffee table strewn with old magazines, sofas pining for better days, and a harsh, sourceless light, the cruel illumination of purgatory.

Mrs. Bath left us on the sofa and went to fetch her husband. By now Audrey's face was red and her breathing was an agony of effort, shaking her small frame. A wheeze that made my ribs ache underlined her every inhalation.

Mrs. Bath returned with her husband, a stout, balding man. He shook my hand and said, "Yes, I am Dr. Bath. And this is your wife, the emergency?"

We both looked at Audrey, and I said, "Yes." The doctor wore a black suit and seemed disappointed, although whether this was because Audrey didn't look like emergency enough or looked like more emergency than he had bargained for, I couldn't tell.

Mrs. Bath helped Audrey up from the sofa where she was hunched forward in private communication with her lungs. Flanked by the doctor and his wife, Audrey was led past the reception desk toward the hall. Something in their progress, their tentative exit, put me in mind of two skaters guiding a novice across the ice.

I waited on the sofa while the doctor and Mrs. Bath attended my wife. I shuffled through the magazines on the coffee table, seeking something to occupy my mind, but I was certain I didn't want to read anything about infants or celebrities or health or crafts, and I was growing irritated with this foraging when—I found my Muse!

My Muse resided within the unlikely confines of a thin, battered paperback entitled *Pilgrim at Tinker Creek* by someone named Annie Dillard. I noted a number of laudatory blurbs on the back and began reading. I had no premonition, no shiver of recognition on opening the book, that my inspiration would lie within.

I was instantly intrigued. So engrossed was I that I did not notice Audrey standing over me, flanked again by the doctor and his wife. All three were smiling. Audrey's smile was weak, relieved more than celebratory, but it lifted my heart.

I wrote a check for $85 while the doctor talked. He was more animated now, hearty and pleased with himself. "Your wife, she has the spider bite!" he said. "Right there on the ankles. Hah! Or maybe the bee sting or a, what you call, centepeeder? Not everyone are allergic. Most, they just say, 'Ow!' and forget about it." Here the doctor shrugged to indicate a cavalier attitude toward such attacks. "But your wife, she has the reactions, so I give her the shot and these pills, samples while the drugstore does not open. Problems? You must call."

I asked Mrs. Bath if I might have the paperback I was holding in my hand, and she sold it to me for five dollars, which seemed a little steep. I didn't haggle.

Driving back to our home, slowly, keeping an eye out for nocturnal creatures that might race from the surrounding woods and hurl themselves beneath our wheels, I could not contain my enthusiasm.

"I know what I'm going to write," I told Audrey. She turned her head, her cheek flat against the backrest, her red hair matted in thick ribbons. She was clearly exhausted, and she regarded me with blue eyes that were uncharacteristically blank. Ordinarily, Audrey would have expressed delight, urged me to elaborate, but she wasn't up to it that night. I understood, and I should have left it till morning, but I couldn't contain the good news.

"I am going to write essays! Nature essays. You know, thoughtful pieces in which nature serves as a sort of jumping off place for larger topics. Caterpillar-to-butterfly stuff about transformation, a little something from Ovid or Hazlitt or Burton thrown in. 'The world is but a school for inquiry,' after all. So. We've got a classroom in our own backyard! Our property has woods, a pond, a small creek. I haven't seen the creek yet, but the real estate agent said it was there, no reason to doubt her. And here we are in April, everything coming alive. 'When that April with his shoures soote the droghte of March hath perced to the roote,' that sort of thing."

Audrey rolled her eyes, snorted derisively.

"What?" I asked.

My wife exhaled (the tiniest trace of a wheeze still there) and looked at me as though I'd just announced that I intended to run for president.

"What? I think the essay is the perfect vehicle for my temperament and—"

"Nature, Jonathan. What do you know about nature?"

"Well." I was caught off balance by this attack, so unlike my wife. I realized later that Audrey was speaking in the immediate aftermath of a life-threatening encounter with a tiny piece of nature. No wonder she was unenthusiastic regarding my new allegiance. At the time, however, I was hurt.

"I believe I have a layman's knowledge of the natural world," I said, hating the prissy tightness in my throat.

"No one would ever describe you as an outdoors person," Audrey said.

"I don't believe I need to be climbing mountains or rafting down the Amazon to write about nature."

"No," Audrey said. "I don't suppose so. But you need...." She paused. She stretched the tip of her tongue to touch her upper lip, a habit she had when looking within, and one I generally found endearing. She smiled. "Name three trees."

"What?"

"Come on, name three trees. That's an easy one."

Yes, an easy one, insultingly so, beneath reply. Mistaking my silence for ignorance, her smile enlarged, so I snapped back, "Juniper, Christmas, Mimosa!" and she continued to grin, as though she had won somehow, and I found myself fretting that juniper might be, technically, more of a shrub than a tree. But I wasn't going to have my Muse belittled by continuing the conversation. I changed the subject.

"I'm glad you are all right," I said.

"Not as glad as I am," she said, which probably meant nothing, but it felt like a rebuke. I drove the rest of the way in silence, and when we pulled into our yard, Audrey said, "All out for Walden."

In spite of my wife's sarcasm, I was convinced that the essay was the form for me. For one thing, I was wealthy. With wealth came leisure, and leisure encouraged reflection. It occurred to me that one of the great charms of the essay was this conveyed sense that its author had all the time in the world. The authors of essays drifted in a fog of indolence, contemplating objects and events, pursuing literary allusions with scholarly languor. The average reader, hustling to get his car to the Jiffy Lube on his lunch hour, could only dream of some faraway retirement when time would cease to flog him with errands and obligations. To read an essay was to enter a world of literary and philosophical loafing, to wade in that slow river of time. Readers of essays could, for the span of the piece, escape their deadline days.

I had every confidence that I could give the reader his money's worth in reflection, but I thought I might have trouble with the nature part. While I didn't feel I was as ill equipped for the job as Audrey believed, it is true I never had warmed to nature as a child. I never had an urge to climb a tree, own a turtle, look under a log, or catch a fish. I wasn't immune to the beauty of autumn, with hills transformed by garish yellows and reds, and spring, with its thousand shades of green, was a wonder of renewal, no doubt about it, but I didn't wish for any deeper connection. In fact, I had always kept a cool distance from the natural world, which I perceived as deadly and erratic, the rotting rabbit by the side of the road, festering with maggots, the yellow jackets that buzzed around the picnic table, climbing down the throat of the open Coke bottle.

Nature could be hostile, as Bob, of Bob's Bug and Vermin Blasters, reminded me. Audrey and I had decided to purge the house of bugs to prevent a second occurrence of that harrowing night, and Bob's Bug and Vermin Blasters was the only local establishment for such services.

Bob was a large man outfitted in olive drab camouflage, his pants stuffed into gray rubber boots. He had laughed, an incredulous, seal-like sound muffled by his mustache, when

Audrey had expressed her reservations regarding the contents of the canister that he intended to spray inside and outside the house.

"Yes, ma'am," he said. "This here is deadly poison. That's a fact. Might be you want something organic." His eyes, bright blue and winking out from under bushy eyebrows, showed deep amusement. "Just sprinkle some garlic on the bastards. Or say a prayer. You know what the word *organic* means to a bug? It means *dinner*."

Bob made more seal sounds. Audrey turned and left the room without saying anything, and I accompanied Bob on his rounds, watched him go through the house, crawling under the kitchen sink, squirting death behind the refrigerator, in the cupboards, along the baseboards. When he headed off to the basement, I left him to his work and went outside. I sat on the porch reading some more of the Dillard book until Bob came outside and I tagged along again, watching him as he drilled deep holes into the cinder block and squirted poison into the holes. All the while, he supplied me with a wealth of anecdotal material about his trade. "Ants are mad about electricity," he said. "I've known them to eat the insulation off wires. I've found dead clumps of them in air conditioning units and around electrical terminals. All the lights go off in your house, it could be ants feeding their addiction. And the thing about ants, the thing about a lot of bugs, is they don't give a goddam whether they live or die. That's an edge they got in the war. And you might think war's an exaggeration for it, but I've been in the business a long time, and war's the word. And there ain't a clear winner yet."

When Bob had finished with the house, he said, "I'll just mosey around the property, see if there's any problems brewing, maybe a big hive. There's a hell of a lot to be said for a preemptive strike." I watched him set out toward the woods, the canister balanced on his shoulder, an American warrior, and I went back in for dinner.

Audrey was sitting in the kitchen, her elbows planted on the table, a book open before her. I looked over her shoulder and experienced a shock. She was reading *For Whom the Bell Tolls*. I just stood and stared until she sensed my presence, turned around and looked up.

"What?"

"I thought you hated Hemingway?"

Audrey looked a little sheepish, then defiant. "He has hardly any commas."

I raised my eyebrows in query.

"I can't handle commas right now," she said. "I can't breathe on a comma. And Henry James...all those commas. I nearly fainted trying to catch my breath."

I didn't know what to say, so I just nodded my head and moved on to the refrigerator. In retrospect, I guess it was a warning I should have heeded. But retrospect and two dollars and fifty cents will get you a latte at Starbucks.

That night I was reading in bed when I heard an engine cough into life. I knew it wasn't someone making off with our Camry; that would have been a different sound entirely. This was the distinctive rattle of a diesel engine in need of a tune-up. I slipped out of bed, taking care not to wake Audrey, and went to the window in time to see red taillights curve down the driveway and disappear past the trees. I realized that I had just seen Bob leaving in his truck. I had forgotten entirely about Bob. I looked at my watch. It was ten minutes past midnight. I marveled at such dedication. Say what you will about country folk, their work ethic is admirable, an example for the rest of us.

I returned to the bed and decided that I'd better get some sleep myself. Tomorrow I planned to confront nature, armed with a notepad, a pencil, and a will to revel in her wonders, no matter how stony the soil, how overgrown the path.

As I moved toward the bed, Audrey stirred in her sleep, stretched and turned on her side, rolling the bed sheet with her and pulling it up past her feet. I bent to pull it back down and noticed something on her ankle, a pale green patch of light. I leaned closer. Between her ankle and her heel, an area of skin the size of a quarter glowed with the yellow-green luminosity of a night clock's hands. As I studied this glowing spot, it dimmed and disappeared. *Odd*, I thought. I pulled the covers over her feet, resolving to mention it in the morning. I remembered that the spider or mite or whatever had launched its assault on her ankle. No doubt this was a related effect, nothing to worry about. Still, it might signify the onslaught of infection. Audrey might not be aware of the phenomenon if it only manifested itself in the dark. Another consultation with Dr. Bath might be in order.

I slept poorly and dreamed that I was back at Clayton teaching a class on biology, and Francis Bacon had come to demonstrate to my students just how to stuff a chicken with snow, this being the famous experiment that had led to his death by pneumonia. I found myself disliking Bacon, who was pompous and rude and wearing an ugly blue dress, and I asked him to leave and he took a swing at me with the chicken, but then the dream's logic broke down, and the chicken, while still looking like a chicken, was much larger, was, in fact, my old high school drama teacher, Mrs. Unger, and I woke up. It took me half an hour to get back to sleep, and the sleep I gleaned was shallow, the dregs of rest.

I wasn't feeling entirely fit in the morning, but I probably would have remembered to mention the ankle business after my first cup of coffee. Audrey, no more of a morning person than I, lumbered down from the bathroom where her morning ablutions had taken an inordinately long time. I looked at her and was…well, puzzled.

We men know that sometimes the women in our lives will look different. I can't speak for all men, but I know that I have an uncanny sensitivity to this new-look thing. I become instantly alert, like a deer in the forest on hearing the snap of a twig. New hair style? New lipstick, new eye shadow? Is this alteration for my benefit? Is a compliment in order? It can be a panicky moment. Not all new looks are planned or, if planned, executed with success. If some new hair style is, in Audrey's opinion, a great disaster, or if—an early learning experience—she has simply slept funny on her hair, producing a fuzzy, disheveled effect, a compliment can precipitate tears.

I was more baffled than usual. Audrey looked like Audrey and then again, quite different. She seemed to have a higher forehead, a just-scrubbed look, a nakedness of feature and a new bluntness to her gaze.

Audrey is very intuitive, and we have been married for ten years—we were married just after we got our undergraduate degrees—so she sensed my confusion.

"Eyebrows," she said.

"Excuse me?"

"I shaved off my eyebrows. I was looking at myself in the mirror, and, I don't know, they looked superfluous."

I had one of those revelations that, despite several bad experiences, I always share. "Like commas!" I said.

"What?"

"Well, eyebrows are sort of like commas, and you've been having this thing about commas, not liking them."

"That's the craziest thing I've ever heard," Audrey said.

"Is it?" I jumped up, ran into the living room, and returned with *For Whom the Bell Tolls*. I plopped the book down in front of her and flipped the pages.

"Okay, I'm crazy. What's this?" Every comma had been sliced with a short red line, that little mincing flourish that is the copy editor's delete symbol. There were a lot of red deletes, more than I would have expected in Hemingway.

Audrey stood up suddenly and snatched the book from the table, clutching it to her chest. "A marriage is not an invitation to abuse another person's privacy."

"It's just a book; it's not your diary."

Audrey sniffed. "And I suppose that *The Great Gatsby* is just a book?"

She had me there. My copy of *The Great Gatsby* is a very personal, passionately annotated book, and I had thrown—I winced to remember—a fit when I had found Audrey reading it.

"You're right," I said. "I'm sorry. I'm a lout. I don't know how you put up with me."

Audrey is not one to hold a grudge, and we hugged each other and kissed.

I drank the rest of my coffee standing up. I set the mug down, grabbed my backpack, and moved to the door. "Today's the big day, off into the wilderness to bag some inspiration."

"Yes, I can see. Good luck." Audrey wiggled her fingers at me.

Then I was out the door and walking across the tall grass toward a pale meadow and the vibrant green of the trees beyond. I was a little nervous, so much seemed to ride on this venture. Did I really have the stuff it took to be an essayist?

I had made preparations for the journey (journey may be too extravagant a word for an outing that doesn't leave home). I wore heavy khaki pants, hiking boots, a long-sleeved flannel shirt, a backpack containing a first-aid kit, a packed lunch (baloney sandwich, apple, cheese), a flashlight, a spade, two jars for specimens, several balls of twine, my notepad and pencils, a pocket knife, a compass, and a bottle of spring water.

I entered the meadow. The straw-colored grass reached to my waist. I ignored the disquiet that came with a sudden sense of vulnerability. The pale blue sky loomed over me, tattered scraps of cloud moving slowly, animated by the same wind that stirred the grass. *Waves of amber*, I thought, pleased with the metaphor, then chagrined, realizing that the image wasn't original.

But I was getting the hang of this, marching along, my initial trepidation eased by the comforting weight of the sun on my neck and shoulders.

The gods lie in wait for the overly confident, and just as I was loosening up, living in the moment, something exploded in front of me with a great whirring and fury, a brown blur aimed at my head, and I stumbled backward and fell, my heart banging around in my chest.

I scrambled back up and saw a bird flapping its way to the clouds. I remembered a movie I had seen in which hunters with shotguns and dogs had hunted birds—were they called wrens? That doesn't seem quite it—in a meadow like this, the birds blasting out of the ground with the same *whup-whup-whup* sound that I had just experienced.

I was briskly heading back to the house as I thought this, my rational mind trying to retake the higher ground. I scolded my inner coward. *Are you going to let a blasted bird send you running?*

I continued on course to the house, but I managed, by an act of will, to veer right and down a hill toward the small pond and the clump of sentinel willows—there's another tree, Audrey—and by the time I reached the muddy, weed-strewn bank, I was breathing heavily but relatively calm again. Thoreau got a lot of mileage out of a pond, and I saw no reason why I couldn't squeeze some fine writing out of my own pond. Unfortunately, up close, its charms diminished. The pond had no precise boundary, at least not where I came upon it. Green weeds marched into the water, which was filmed with a yellow-green scum. When I stirred this with a stick, the end of the stick came away with fleshy, dripping blobs of goo. My research brought me too close to the edge, and I was suddenly ankle deep in black, stinking mud, flailing my arms to keep from falling forward, yanking my hiking boots free with rude popping noises while a primal sound of disgust came unbidden from my throat. Small gnats buzzed up in a peppery cloud and rushed at my mouth, nose, and eyes with suicidal abandon (*they don't give a goddam whether they live or die*, I heard Bob saying).

That did it for the day, and I headed back to the house, depressed and angry with myself. I found Audrey on the porch in the rattan chair. Her head was down as she wrote furiously on a legal pad, and when I hailed her, she looked up, smiled abstractedly, and returned to her writing. Her industry seemed a reprimand.

I didn't give up, didn't let nature win the game in the first encounter. Every day I would arise, drink my coffee in the kitchen, kiss Audrey on her forehead—there was something endearing in her eyebrowless state, a subtext speaking volumes on humanity's restless experimental spirit—and I would set off into the wilderness.

I grew comfortable with the pond and the meadow. I was no longer spooked by birds or apt to let mud demoralize and defeat me. I sprayed myself with liberal amounts of insect repellant—Audrey said I smelled like poisonous oranges, even after a shower—and the hordes of hovering midges, mosquitoes and gnats kept their distance. I grew less fastidious. My gag reflex relented. I could pick a tick off my sleeve with nonchalance and expertly crush it between my fingernails, flicking it away. If I thought that the blood on my fingers might be my own, siphoned from me by the creature, I felt only a satisfied sense of revenge, no horror-induced queasiness.

But I was troubled. Despite this new ease, I found no subject for my essay, nothing that spoke my name. I began to have doubts that I ever would, and I was trying to escape an unsettling conclusion: Nature was boring. Turtles sat on logs soaking up the rays of the sun, as listless and devoid of interest as a pile of dirty socks. They'd sit so maddeningly still that I'd be compelled to hurl rocks at them until they showed some life by flopping into the pond and disappearing. And that, in itself, wasn't wildly entertaining. Nature's infinite variety was beginning to look like a rut. If you thought about it, even the seasons, rolling around every year in the same damned order (spring, summer, fall, winter, spring, summer, fall, winter), suggested a dearth of imagination. The pond was stupefied with routine. Fish endlessly rose to dimple the pond's demeanor while small, sunflower-seed creatures with wire-thin legs skipped pointlessly across the water's surface. Bugs whirred over the weeds; small round birds darted down from the willow trees to eat them again and again and again.

I wasn't ready to give up, but I was having my doubts, my crisis of faith. I decided that the woods, still unexplored, might be my salvation.

I had been reluctant to enter the woods. There is a primal fear of nature when it closes ranks. Dante's dark wood is a place where only the lost find themselves. Who would seek it out?

The night I resolved to enter the woods the next morning was the same night that Audrey shared several pages of her manuscript with me. She was burning with the fever of creation, moving around the living room as she read, gesturing dramatically with her free hand. Her hair, cropped short with a scissors and wild abandon, was a red, spiky flag of rebellion that would have won my heart had she not already owned it.

It became apparent, as Audrey read these fresh pages, that her physical appearance didn't mark the full extent of her experimentation. She had discovered a new approach to the memoir, a surreal language that captured the dissociative state produced by abuse.

I confess I couldn't follow it all. I did not recognize all of the words (Latin? Joycean synthesis?) and the narrative was disjointed. As soon as Audrey finished reading, she flopped down on the sofa and began writing furiously on her legal pad, not waiting for my response. I didn't disturb her or try to take the loose pages from her so that I could conduct a more careful reading. I doubt she would have let me. She almost never relinquished a work-in-progress for my scrutiny. I got up and went into the study where I wrote down the sentence that I had committed to memory, but even as I wrote the words, I distrusted their accuracy. This is what I wrote: "My brood brother committed the sin of threes and had no smoothness so that I wished he had splintered into *hoosith hostoth* [?] and I was shamed by my parent wheel and uttered an asymmetrical harmony that generated sadness back to the last *falofath* [?] where the latent ones hooted and sent their sound-scents throughout the burrow."

You can understand why I can't vouch for the accuracy of my transcription. But I think that does capture the tone.

I set out with a will the next morning, spurred on by a new competitive spirit. I didn't want Audrey to leave me in her literary dust.

I tied the free end of the string around the trunk of a tree and let the ball unravel as I entered the woods, stepping gingerly over logs and avoiding the larger, more formidable clumps of vegetation. Far from the menace I had imagined, I felt an immediate sense of serenity. Light fell through the overhead canopy of leaves, dappling the mossy ground with green, shifting shapes. Aside from a few birds scraping around in the bushes and the faraway chittering of an insect or bird or frog, there was a sweet, almost reverent hush. I inhaled the rich scent of earthy decay and the green life that fed on it.

I was pleased with myself for thinking up the ball-of-twine trick. I could simply follow the string back, winding it around the cardboard core as it returned me to the meadow. I had several balls of string, so I could easily extend my range by tying the end of one to the beginning of the next. And, as a failsafe measure, I had a compass and had ascertained on the map that I could march east for less than a mile and discover the dirt road that ran parallel to my property and that would lead me back to my house.

I expected that days, perhaps weeks, would be needed to scout this woods as methodically as I had explored the pond and meadow, but on my first day I found the creek and, following it northward, encountered a clearing and the creatures that were to be my subject, creatures so fascinating, so complex in their behavior, that they promised a whole book of essays.

I had come upon the clearing at midday, stepping into full sunlight from under the arch of a fallen tree, dazed, delighted, charmed. My creek, which had seemed, in the shadow of the forest, rather too dark and slippery for close inspection, was transformed. Now as lively and lovely as something from a fairy tale, it ran glittering through the middle of this verdant swale.

I proceeded to unpack my lunch and eat it, sitting on the green grass and smiling at my surroundings. Having been disappointed by my meadow and its forlorn pond, I had lowered my expectations, and this clearing, with its picture-book beauty, was a fine surprise, a reward, perhaps, for pushing on. I quoted Rilke to the air: "The earth is like a child that knows poems."

While eating my lunch, I became aware of a steady low drone that filled the air. The sound was like nothing I had heard before. Most of nature's noises confirmed my belief that nature was just going through the motions: the repetitive *Whatever, Whatever, Whatever* of a bird that had lost its

mind or the mechanical buzz of thousands of insects in thrall
to a numbing need to procreate. But the sound that filled my
ears in that clearing carried a profound emotional content, as
though all the inhabitants of a great monastery were mourn-
ing the loss of paradise.

On finishing my lunch, I wadded up the paper bag and
thrust it into my backpack. In my forays into the wilds, I had
been delighted to find that this action was reflexive. I am
sure no author of nature essays litters.

I had the instincts for my calling. I now employed those
instincts to locate this poignant chant that so intrigued me.
At first the sound seemed generalized, permeating the air,
but I determined that it came from the creek, more specifi-
cally from that portion of the creek that disappeared into a
thicket of squat shrubs and crooked trees brandishing new,
pale-green leaves.

Carefully, not wishing to make any disturbance that
would alert the maker of the sound, I pushed through thorny
underbrush, crawling on my hands and knees like a soldier
behind enemy lines.

I could not have come upon them from a better angle
had I planned it knowing their location. I peered from
behind a screen of leafy vines and was rewarded with my first
view of the crayfish, perhaps fifteen of them scurrying in and
out of their burrows on the opposite bank.

I did not know, then, that they were crayfish. Later that
evening I called Harry Ackermann, and he supplied me with
the name. Harry taught biology at Clayton and had been
doing so for many decades. I caught him at home, and he was
in a hurry to get back to his bridge game where the possibilities for a grand slam invested his voice with an excitement I
had never heard before (dear God, how our lives narrow in
the home stretch).

I described the creatures and would have supplied what I knew of their habits from this first encounter, but Harry cut me off. "They're not insects," he said. "They are crustaceans, crayfish. That's the only freshwater animal that fits your description. That armor you are describing is an exoskeleton. The—" I could hear someone hollering in the background, a shrill female voice that I recognized as belonging to old Dean Winfrey Podner, a lesbian according to student legend which I found fanciful for it required thinking of the dean in sexual terms. "Look, I've got to go," he said and hung up.

I watched my crayfish all that afternoon, retreating only when I became aware of the sinking sun and realized I'd be making my way through the woods in the dark if I didn't call it a day.

Those hours of observation on that first day were strewn with epiphanies. My Muse hugged herself for joy and sang within my head.

The sad hum that filled the air was clearly generated by the crayfish who vibrated in a minor key as they scuttled over the bare clay soil, diving into holes in the bank, leaping in and out of the bright water of the stream.

Sometimes two crayfish would encounter each other, hug, their bodies shivering more rapidly while their antennae waved wildly. Whether this entwining was sexual or served some other function, I couldn't determine. Later I learned that this activity had to do with enlisting other members in what I came to call a *meld*, intending to seek out the proper term at a later date.

Before leaping into the water, the crayfish would remove parts of their armor—what Harry called their exoskeletons—revealing smooth flesh, white as toothpaste, that boiled with tiny tentacles. I would have liked to discuss this removable exoskeleton with Harry and would have broached the subject on the phone had his manner been less abrupt. Was this common to crustaceans, this ability to doff their exoskeletons? I was almost certain that other creatures couldn't do this. Turtles couldn't shed their shells and snails...well, maybe snails could. I mean, that's what slugs are, right?

That evening, when I arrived home, I found Audrey working zealously in the neglected vegetable garden by the side of the house. Neither of us had ever thought to resuscitate this garden, hadn't spoken of it. Audrey didn't like gardens of any kind and had hinted at unpleasant experiences with vegetables in her past, but that evening her face was streaked with black dirt, and her shaved head shone with honest sweat—so few women have the bone structure to carry off a shorn look; Audrey does—and she smiled at me with the pride of a hard day's labor done and, turning away, hefted her hoe again and had at the weeds. I didn't tell her about my crayfish. I wanted to surprise her with the essay.

I entered the house and went straight for the kitchen where I grabbed an apple and a box of crackers. Then it was off to the study and to work. I began my essay:

> We are human and we think in human terms. Draw a line from a stone to a star, from a dinosaur bone to a dead ant, and wherever the lines intersect, there lies the human heart. Are we hopelessly self-referential or does the world truly speak to us?
>
> It is easy to relate to those clear similarities, those echoes of our own mortal condition. The gorilla in his cage induces guilt when we look into his eyes. We see ourselves. The dead raccoon induces the same guilt when, at the wheels of our automobiles, we speed past its carcass, tossed negligently to the side of the road. We see our own unhappy ends. But what of smaller, more

elusive creatures whose suffering is largely hidden from us? What of the low moan of little things? Can that really be grief we hear or is it an accident, harmonies with another purpose that fall upon our human ears and take the shape of sadness? I speak of the lonesome song of the crayfish, that song that the wind carries to us, that sound that seems encoded with loss and despair.

I was very pleased with that beginning, so pleased that I couldn't continue. Art should never be hurried, particularly the essay with its obligatory andante. Besides, I needed more familiarity with my subject, more detail to support my reflective voice.

As the weeks went by I was reminded of the danger of confusing the metaphor with what it illustrates. I was so fascinated by these crayfish that I often lost the essayist in the amateur naturalist.

But I think I always regained the higher ground, and, in all humility, I think these passages demonstrate that:

> When I witness crayfish melding, generally in twelves or nines, more rarely in sixes, I am always amazed at how they fold into a completely new organism. The mega-crayfish seems to defy its origins, to heroically turn its back on the past. Single crayfish eat their exoskeletons before the meld, knowing there is no going back, demonstrating a selflessness that human societies might find admirable.
>
> The first time I observed a mega-crayfish I had come upon it after the meld. I thought I was seeing a different animal entirely, although not one I was familiar with. The mega-crayfish comes in a variety

of shapes, and this one looked something like a cat-sized spider except that it had a great many more legs than a spider and moved by collapsing a number of legs and falling in that direction, creating an odd, rollicking form of locomotion. This one dove into the water and returned with a frog which, I assumed, it was going to eat. Instead, it took the frog apart, peeling the skin back and plucking out various organs which it handed to the mendicant crayfish surrounding it. This was unpleasant to watch, since the frog continued to struggle throughout the operation, and the mega-crayfish performed the dissection with slow, finicky care. I expected the waiting crayfish to devour the morsels they had received from the mega-crayfish, and perhaps they did, but they did this out of my sight, disappearing into their holes with their treasures.

After the skeleton had been dismantled and carried away, when the frog was nothing more than a sheath of mottled skin, the mega-crayfish offered this last remnant to the last waiting crayfish, who took the skin, donned it like a Halloween cape, and dashed toward his hole with a fleetness that seemed powered by joy.

And then, of course, the mega-crayfish dismantled itself, pinching off its legs, unraveling its innards, and collapsing, finally, in a rubble of black exoskeleton, yellow blood and emerald guts. I expect this ritual has been observed by countless generations of country boys who give it no more thought than they might give to the birth of a calf or a bat caught in a sister's hair, but I must say, coming upon this gruesome spectacle with no warning of what was about to occur…it was unsettling, to say the least.

Perhaps it was the mega-crayfish's nature to tear itself apart; perhaps it was born to dissect and, lacking a subject, dissected itself. The analogy is easy, almost too easy: We human creatures deconstruct the universe and are left in the rubble of our fears, our mortality, our rags of faith.

I was pleased with that passage, and if Audrey had seen me at that moment, she might have said, as was her wont, "You look like you've just won the lottery."

But Audrey was nowhere around. She was probably upstairs reading in bed. I went outside and sat in the rocking chair and looked at the stars (Hopkins's "fire-folk sitting in the air") and thought that there were a lot of them in Pennsylvania, and I thought about how I might become very famous and hounded by fans. I might have to hire security guards or at least get a dog although I wasn't sure about getting a fierce dog because what if it began looking at me funny, started growling deep in its throat?

I sent the future marching, took a deep breath and rocked in the moment. I noticed that the night was very still. All the world's raucous frogs were silent, not a peep.

As the days continued to pass, the exploits of my crayfish kept feeding my essay, and it grew to an unwieldy size. It was beginning to show its ignorance, by which I mean that my lack of scientific knowledge regarding these crustaceans was becoming a problem. No doubt there was a scientific term for what I called a meld. And what was occurring when two crayfish fought and the loser erupted in flames? The power of the image suggested a host of wonderful references throughout history and literature, but if I knew the mechanism—some volatile chemical released in defeat?—I could speak with more authority, send a telling anecdote or literary reference straight to the heart of the matter.

I needed to read up on crayfish. My decision was made on a Thursday evening after dinner. Scanning the phone book, which contained four counties and was still thinner than a copy of *The New Yorker*, I discovered—I confess I was surprised—a library in our very town. I thought it might still be open.

The parking lot was empty and dark, and the library, a small, shed-like building, appeared abandoned, although a closer inspection revealed a pale gleam of yellow light edging from beneath the window's drawn shade. I went to the door, turned the knob, and entered. An elderly woman sitting behind her desk jerked her head up as though she had been caught dozing.

"I can summon the police with a touch of a button, young man. There's nothing here but library fines, less than five dollars, not worth the loss of your freedom and good name."

I told her that I was seeking a book about crayfish.

"There are people who eat them," she said. Being a librarian, I suppose she felt obligated to contribute her knowledge on the subject.

"Not me," I said and waited for her to help with the search. She returned with two books, one entitled, *The Flora and Fauna of Western Pennsylvania* and the other a children's book entitled *What's Under That Rock?*

I checked out both books after filling out a library card application that was three pages long and expected me to know things like my mother's maiden name. I lied and got through it and made off with the books.

I intended to retire to the study and read these books immediately, but I saw the message light on the answering machine blinking, and so I pushed the play button and Audrey's voice jumped out. "Jonathan! When you get this, I'll be on my way to the coast with Dr. Bath and his wife. The quantum actualization of the brood wheel has come to us in a vision. It will bloom near San Clemente, and so we are on our way. These other manifestations are important, but they are not the blooming. You can be of use where you are. Please tend to my garden. We will meet again in celebration and the making of fine multiples."

I went into the kitchen, fumbled in the cupboards, and found the bottle of Gilbey's gin. It was my fault she'd left. I'd been neglecting her, lost in my damned essay about those damned crayfish. Neglected, she had fled into a crackpot religion. I should have seen it coming; the signs were there. I mixed the gin with a lemony diet drink that tasted awful. That was fine; I deserved it. Later I walked out into the yard and through the meadow and into the woods. I carried a flashlight and my backpack and trusted the familiarity of the route. There was a full moon, and I was drunk enough to fear no night thing.

I entered the clearing without incident, but I must have drifted from my habitual path, for a resilient sapling caught my leg and threw me to the ground. I turned my flashlight, and the beam revealed a silver rod growing out of the grass. I reached forward and touched the rod and as I gripped it, it began to slide down into itself. This wasn't at all like a sapling, and I studied the rod, pulling it up and then forcing it down again. It was a telescoping antenna. I retrieved my spade from the backpack and dug around the antenna, striking something hard. I brushed away the dirt to reveal a flat metal surface just under the ground. It took me well over two hours to unearth most of the truck's cab. The cab was full of dirt—and Bob. There was black dirt in Bob's mouth, black dirt in his eye sockets. His hands still clutched the wheel, ready to go but...*You lost the war*, I thought, a stupid thought. I was feeling a little ill, and it didn't help, my staring at the grass which grew undisturbed over what had to be the larger bulk of the truck. *How did you get there, Bob?*

I heard the new sound, a sound that did not resonate with loss but seemed joyous, playful, exuberant. I crawled into the thicket and took my station. The full moon provided more than enough illumination, but I could have seen them without it, for each crayfish was enveloped in a pale green glow. They were running in and out of a fine spray of mist, for all the world like children squealing and frolicking in the spray of a hose or water sprinkler. I recognized the source of the spray, Bob's deadly canister of poison. Three of the crayfish operated it from its dug-in position high in the bank, while a dozen or more raced in and out of the toxic mist.

As always, I was entranced, and I might have crouched there watching them for hours, but something moved behind them, a shadow that shifted and, for a moment, eclipsed the moon and flooded my heart with terror. I scrambled out of the thicket, stood upright, and ran.

I stumbled through the woods, crashing into trees, toppling over logs, but always up again and moving. The meadow left me unprotected; I imagined malevolent eyes watching me from above. I ran.

I reached the porch as my stomach cramped. I eased myself down on the first porch step and blinked at the silvered grass, the meadow and the trees beyond. The spinning world wobbled to a stop as I caught my breath. Peace reigned; the stars were noncommittal and the breeze was warm and quick with the promise of spring. I glanced down at Audrey's garden and thought of going after her, but Audrey wouldn't like that. No, time would have to bring her back to me...*the fullness of time* (a phrase that seemed suddenly sinister; I saw this monstrous thing, bloated with the eons it had devoured).

No going after Audrey. Hadn't she charged me with the care of her garden? She had taken pains with this project, covering the ground with plastic sheets to protect the new shoots from the vicissitudes of the season. I stood up and regarded one of the sheets. I looked over my shoulder, but nothing was coming. I knelt down and peeled back the sheet and saw rows of neatly ordered little plants, white buds with blue...No. My mind was forced to swallow the image, but it had no response ready-made. Indeed, my first reaction was to laugh abruptly, which really wasn't appropriate. What I saw were rows of little blue eyeballs, naked, unblinking, incredulous. I had never seen a garden that looked so very, very surprised.

I had no time to pursue that thought, for I turned again, prompted by a trumpeting roar that rattled my heart in its cage. The thing was silhouetted against the moon, its ragged wings outstretched, strange tentacles dangling from its black bulk, tentacles long enough to trail across the meadow as though trolling the amber waves.

I am locked in my room now, devising a plan or preparing to devise a plan or, perhaps, simply eating this bag of potato chips and reading. When all is said and done, I enjoy reading far more than writing. Not that I'm very fond of *The Flora and Fauna of Western Pennsylvania*. It has no pictures and it has that shiny paper that I associate with textbooks and the prose is almost impenetrable, and *you know what?* I'm an adult, and I don't have to read it if I don't want to. Hah.

Well, *What's Under That Rock?* is a great improvement. For one thing, it has pictures. A picture is worth a thousand words. There's a picture of a crayfish in this book.

Something is on the roof...make that *in the attic*. The noise doesn't conjure a clear picture in my mind. Visualize a half dozen sailors, brawling while someone tortures a pig. No. I think you have to be here to fully appreciate this sound.

I keep looking at this drawing of a crayfish. *Cambarus bartoni*, that's its scientific name. It looks *exactly* like a tiny lobster. That's simple enough, isn't it? I mean, what kind of genius do you have to be to say, "Jonathan, those aren't crayfish. I don't know what the hell they are, but they aren't crayfish. *Crayfish look exactly like small lobsters*"? Is that so difficult?

Thanks a lot, Harry Ackermann. I hope your grand slam fizzled.

"When sorrows come, they come not single spies, but in battalions." You are so right, Will.

I'm just sick, really sick and disgusted. *And the essay is ruined, of course.*